THE GLIMMERWOOD KEY

NICHOLAS FROST

TABLE OF CONTENTS

DEDICATION

For those who see the magic not in the shout, but in the silence.

And for my own quiet things, wherever you may be.

AUTHOR'S NOTE

A Note on Quiet Things

Dear Reader,

For many years, my greatest joy has been writing stories like "The Boy Who Saved Christmas" stories built on the wonder of grand gestures, warm hearths, and the joyful noise of belonging. But every good story requires the space *between* the sound.

The Glimmerwood Key is a novel dedicated to the wisdom of that quiet space. It asks us to look closely at what we choose to forget—the lost memories, the small heartbreaks, the feelings that grow cold in the empty corners of our lives. Through Arthur Pensive, I wanted to explore what happens when you stop trying to fix the world with noise and start healing it with attention.

The most profound magic, I've learned, often isn't the loudest. It's the one that exists right here, right now, humming in the background of your own quiet life. Thank you for listening.

Nicholas Frost

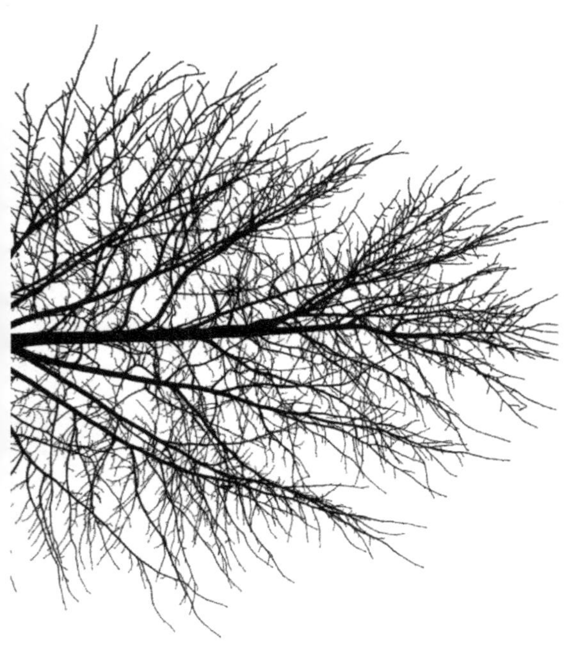

PROLOGUE
THE FIRST QUIET

Before sound, there was silence.

It was a silence so profound that it wasn't an absence of noise, but the absolute fullness of pure possibility. This original, teeming stillness was the birthplace of all that would ever be remembered.

But existence, once begun, is messy. It creates echoes: sounds that reverberate, memories that cling, and songs that stop unfinished. And so, the stillness realized it needed a purpose. It needed a counterweight to keep the chaos from consuming the stories, and to ensure the stories themselves did not become stagnant, suffocating the possibility of new life.

From this need came the Balance.

The great forces were established: The Remembering and

The Forgetting.

And holding them both, sustaining the space between the light and the dark, was the quiet, unwavering awareness of the Foundation.

This Balance is not maintained by magic wands or great armies. It is tended by a listener. It is preserved by a Warden, one who knows that the quietest things—a smooth stone, a broken watch, a simple shared glance—are, in the end, the most powerful truths of all.

Now, listen closely. The first step begins with a boy who thought his greatest flaw was his silence.

The world, for Arthur Pensive, was a museum of quiet things, and he was its solitary curator. His collection was not one of stamps or coins, but of subtle textures, lingering sounds, and the faint, emotional patina that time left on objects. In his pocket, he carried a smooth, grey river stone, worn perfectly oval by centuries of water. In his school desk, a single, moulted blue jay feather lay hidden, its vanes a silent masterpiece of structural engineering. On the sill of his dusty attic bedroom, a rusted bolt from an abandoned railway line sat like a tiny, stubborn monument to decay.

This unique curation was his defense against the noise.

At Lakeland Middle School, Arthur was a ghost. He navigated the bustling hallways like a stationary object in a strong current, the shouts, locker slams, and pop music parting around him without ever truly touching him. He wasn't bullied—that would require attention his peers were unwilling to grant. He was simply... overlooked. His teachers' eyes slid past him in class, landing always on more vocal students. His name was a label on a filing cabinet, not a call to engagement.

The cafeteria was the worst. It was a cacophony of belonging, a roaring marketplace of social currency where Arthur had nothing to trade. He always sat at the same isolated table, near the overflowing recycling bins, shielded by a book. Today's volume was on geology, but the words swam before his eyes. The real drama was the room's deep, ambient hum: the frantic, shallow energy shimmering beneath the popular kids' loud laughter, and the quiet desperation of the other solitary outliers. The very walls seemed to pulse with the accumulated stress of a thousand forgotten tests and social dramas.

"Pensive! Living up to your name again?"

The voice, loud and laced with casual cruelty, belonged to Liam Carter. Liam didn't just exist in the noise; he was one of its chief architects. He loomed over Arthur's table, flanked by his usual court.

Arthur didn't look up from his book. "It's just my name, Liam."

"Looks like you're about to cry into your sandwich," Liam sneered, jabbing a finger at Arthur's lunch. "What's even in there? Gruel?"

It was a perfectly normal ham and cheese sandwich. But under Liam's mocking gaze, it felt suddenly absurd, a testament to Arthur's profound ordinariness. Arthur felt his face grow hot. He focused on the wood grain of the tabletop, imagining it as a miniature landscape of impassable canyons and ridges, a world he could instantly vanish into.

"Leave him alone, Liam."

The voice was quiet but firm. It came from Anya Sharma, who sat two tables over, her nose typically buried in a sketchbook. She didn't look up, just continued to shade a complex drawing of a dragon. Her intervention was as minimal and effective as a precise pencil stroke. It was enough. Liam, deprived of a satisfying reaction, snorted and moved on, his satellites jostling after him.

Anya spared Arthur a fractional glance—a look that wasn't pity, but something closer to recognition. Then she looked away. The moment passed. Arthur's clenched heart slowly relaxed. He gave a small, almost imperceptible nod in her direction, which she may or may not have seen. It was the most resonant social interaction he'd had all week.

The walk home was his sanctuary. He took the long way, through the overgrown park at the neighborhood's edge. Here, the noise faded, replaced by the rustle of oak leaves and the chatter of sparrows. He stopped by his favorite bench, its green paint flaking away to reveal the silver-grey wood beneath. He ran his fingers over the carved initials—"J.L. + R.M. 1973." A promise, or perhaps a heartbreak, frozen in time. He could almost feel the ghost of it, a faint, bittersweet echo that resonated with his own solitude.

Home was a different kind of quiet. A large Victorian house that held its silence like a long, held breath. His mother, Dr. Eleanor Pensive, would be in her study, the door firmly closed, the only sign of her presence the relentless, muted tapping of her keyboard as she composed dense academic papers on obscure historical trade routes. His father, Dr. Alistair Pensive, would be in his den, surrounded by schematics, designing efficient ventilation systems for buildings Arthur would never see.

They were not unkind people. They were simply… preoccupied. Their minds were vast, elegant libraries, but their doors were permanently marked "Staff Only." Arthur was a patron allowed to browse, but never to check anything out.

"Hello, Arthur," his mother had said upon his arrival, her eyes never leaving her monitor. "There's leftover pasta in the fridge."

"How was school?" his father had asked later, his gaze fixed on a complex blueprint. The question was a polite formality, like asking about the weather.

"Fine," Arthur had replied to both. The word was a hollow shell that contained none of the cafeteria's humiliation, none of the park's peace.

That evening, driven by a restless need for a different kind of quiet, he climbed the pull-down ladder into the attic. This was his true kingdom. It smelled of dust, old paper, and cedar. Slanting rays of the setting sun pierced the single round window, illuminating dancing motes of dust. Here, memories weren't echoes; they were tangible.

He traced the water stain on the floorboards from a long-ago leak. He opened a trunk filled with his outgrown baby clothes, each tiny sweater a monument to a version of himself he could barely recall. In the far corner, under the eaves where shadows were thickest, was his grandfather's trunk. The leather was dry and cracked, the brass fittings tarnished almost black.

He'd looked through it before, but tonight felt different. The tension from the Liam encounter, the silent exchange with Anya, the emotional vacuum of his evening—it all created a pressure in his chest, a desperate need for something more.

He unbuckled the crumbling straps. Inside, nestled in yellowed tissue paper, was a life reduced to artifacts. A sheaf of letters tied with a faded ribbon. A pair of wire-rimmed spectacles in a hard case. A silver pocket watch, its hands frozen at 11:11. And at the very bottom, lying alone as if it demanded solitude, was the key.

It was heavy, far heavier than it looked, forged from a dark, non-reflective metal that seemed to swallow the dim attic light. Its bow was an intricately carved oak leaf, so detailed he could see the veins. Its stem was long and slender, with teeth that were jagged and unique, like the silhouette of a mountain range he'd never seen.

It was cold. But as his fingers closed around it, a vision, sharp and clear, flashed behind his eyes: *The scent of pine needles baking in the sun. The taste of cold, clear water from a spring. The comforting, solid weight of a hand on his shoulder.* It was a feeling of profound belonging, of a peace so deep it was a physical presence.

The key resonated. And in that moment, alone in the dusty attic, Arthur Pensive resonated back.

CHAPTER TWO

THE THRESHOLD OF WONDER

The key burned in Arthur's palm, a cold fire that sent shivers up his arm. The ghostly sensations of pine and sunlight and that comforting handprint faded, leaving behind an ache of longing so sharp it was physical. He sat there on the dusty attic floorboards for a long time, just staring at it. The mundane sounds of the house—the faint typing, the hum of the refrigerator—felt like an insult, a crude noise trying to drown out a perfect, single note of music.

This was not like the quiet stories whispered by the park bench or the rusted bolt on his sill. This was a shout. A declaration. The key was an object that held its story not as a fading memory, but as an active, pulsing force. It was the most alive thing he had ever held.

He spent the next hour trying it in every lock he could

find. The attic trunk's small brass lock—too big. The old writing desk—the teeth didn't match. The door to his own room—it wouldn't even insert. A frantic, desperate hope began to curdle into a familiar disappointment. It was a key to nowhere. A beautiful, impossible relic, as useless as he felt in the school cafeteria.

Dejected, he shoved it deep into his pocket, its weight a constant, nagging reminder of the brief connection he'd felt. He went through the motions of the evening: pushing pasta around his plate while his parents discussed the migratory patterns of 14th-century artisans, completing his homework with robotic efficiency, and finally claiming exhaustion to retreat.

But he couldn't sleep. The key felt like a secret too big for his skin. He lay in bed, watching the moon trace a path across his floor, the memory of the pine-scented vision clearer than the reality of his blue-checked duvet.

Finally, driven by a compulsion he didn't understand, he slipped out of bed and pulled on a jacket over his pajamas. The house was steeped in a deep, sleeping silence. He crept down the stairs, avoiding the one that creaked, and slipped out the back door into the chill of the night.

The garden was a world transformed. Bathed in monochrome moonlight, it was no longer just an overgrown yard but a mysterious, silver-drenched landscape. The hawthorn bush cast long, claw-like shadows. The forgotten birdbath was a bowl of liquid mercury. And at the bottom, where the property melted into the wild copse of ancient oaks, his grandfather's tree stood as a colossal, dark sentinel against the starry sky.

His feet, bare in their slippers, were soaked by the dew-heavy grass. The air was cold, sharp in his lungs. This was madness. Yet, the pull was undeniable. The key in his pocket seemed to grow warmer, humming against his thigh with a low, magnetic thrum.

He walked toward the great oak, its bark a tapestry of deep fissures and knotted whorls in the moonlight. It felt older than the house, older than the town, a primal being that had witnessed centuries pass in silence. This was the feeling from the key. This was the source.

On an impulse that felt both utterly insane and perfectly right, he took the key from his pocket. It was no longer cold, but warm, almost body-temperature. The carved oak leaf on the bow seemed to catch the moonlight, glowing with a faint, internal silver sheen.

"Please," he whispered, the word a pale puff of steam in the cold air. He wasn't sure who he was talking to—the tree, the key, the universe itself.

He pressed the metal against the roughened bark, right at the base of the trunk where the great roots dove into the earth. He held his breath.

For three heartbeats, nothing happened. The disappointment was a physical blow, colder than the night air. He was a fool. A lonely boy playing make-believe in the moonlight.

Then, a soft click echoed, not through the air, but deep

within the marrow of his bones, a vibration that started in his feet and traveled up his spine. He gasped and stumbled back as the bark beneath the key began to move. It wasn't splitting or cracking. It was reordering itself, the deep grooves and whorls flowing like liquid wood, shifting and realigning. The groans it emitted were not of breaking, but of waking—the deep, resonant sounds of a giant stirring from a long slumber.

When the movement stilled, a keyhole stood out in stark relief against the trunk. It was dark and deep, edged with what looked like solidified moonlight, and it looked as if it had been grown there, a natural part of the tree, waiting for this exact moment.

Trembling so violently he could barely stand, Arthur stepped forward. The key was humming now, a palpable vibration that travelled up his arm and set his teeth on edge. It was a song of welcome, of homecoming. He slid the key into the lock. The fit was perfect, seamless. It felt less like he was inserting a key and more like he was completing a circuit.

He turned it.

The world did not explode. There was no flash of light or roar of magic. Instead, the solid wood within the keyhole simply... dissolved. It didn't vanish; it became a shimmering, liquid surface, like a vertical pool of quicksilver, reflecting not the garden behind him, but a scene that was impossibly, undeniably elsewhere.

Beyond the threshold was a twilight wood, lit by a soft, internal radiance. The trees were immense, their trunks wider than his bedroom, their canopies a tapestry of silver, deep violet, and a gold that seemed to hold its own light. Moss, thick and soft as velvet and glowing with a faint, emerald bioluminescence, clung to everything. The air that drifted out was cold and smelled of damp earth, frost, and something achingly familiar —the scent from the key: pine and pure, forgotten spring water.

Arthur Pensive, collector of unspoken stories, stood at the edge of the loudest, most impossible thing he had ever encountered. His mind, trained on logic and the mundane, screamed at him to run, to dismiss this as a dream.

But his soul, the deep, resonant part of him that listened to stones, knew the truth. This was real. More real than the school cafeteria, more real than the silent dinner table.

He took one last, shaky breath, pulling the damp, familiar air of his own world into his lungs. He thought of Liam's sneer, his mother's distracted smile, his father's absent gaze. Then he looked into the shimmering doorway, at the path of pale, crushed quartz that led into the glowing, impossible forest.

He pulled the key from the lock. The silvery surface of the doorway remained, stable and waiting.

There was no choice to make. The decision had been made the moment he first touched the key.

Clutching the warm metal in his fist, Arthur Pensive, the boy who was a ghost in his own world, stepped through the Threshold.

The transition was instantaneous. One moment, the cold night air of his garden. The next, a profound, living silence that was not an absence of sound, but a presence. The air was cooler, cleaner, filling his lungs with a vitality he'd never known. The distant hum of traffic was gone, utterly severed. In its place was a symphony of quiet: a soft, sighing wind combing through the needles of immense pines, the gentle trickle of water over stone, and beneath it all, that low, resonant hum—the sound of the earth itself dreaming.

He turned. The doorway was still there, a window framing the shockingly ordinary sight of his own dark garden. It looked like a painting from another life, flat and distant. He reached a hand back through the shimmering surface, half-expecting it to meet resistance, but his fingers passed easily into the cool, damp air of his own world. A wave of relief washed over him. He wasn't trapped. He could go back.

Reassured, he turned to face the wood proper, his heart hammering against his ribs not with fear now, but with a soaring, terrifying wonder.

He was here. He was really here.

CHAPTER THREE

THE FOREST OF REMEMBERED THINGS

The first thing Arthur did, once the initial shock had subsided into a trembling, breathless awe, was to simply stand and breathe. He filled his lungs with the Glimmerwood's air—so pure and cold it felt like drinking light. The very atmosphere seemed charged with a gentle energy, a static of potential that pricked his skin. This was no longer a vision. The moss beneath his thin slippers was soft and springy, releasing a faint, sweet scent of peat and vanilla. The pale quartz path crunched with a satisfying, crystalline sound, a noise that was instantly absorbed by the immense, living quiet of the place.

He took tentative steps forward, away from the Threshold. With each stride, the connection to his old world felt more tenuous, as if he were shedding a heavy, ill-fitting coat. The weight of Liam's taunts, the hollow ache of his parents' inattention, the low-grade anxiety of the school hallways—it all began to feel distant, muffled, like a radio playing in another room.

The forest around him was a testament to a beauty his world had forgotten. The trees were not merely large; they were monumental, their scale so vast it recalibrated his sense of self. He was an insect in a cathedral. Their bark was a symphony of greys, silvers, and charcoal blacks, etched with patterns that looked like forgotten languages. High above, the canopy was a living tapestry. Leaves of beaten gold shivered against deep amethyst, while others, the color of a twilight sky, seemed woven from solidified shadow and starlight. The light that filtered down was diffuse and directionless, bathing everything in a perpetual, serene gloaming.

And then he saw the memories.

His first instinct was to duck. A shimmer of intense blue and silver, the size of a dinner plate, hovered just off the path. It wasn't solid, but it warped the air around it like a heat haze, pulsing with a soft, internal light. As he cautiously approached, a wave of powerful, pure emotion washed over him. It was a feeling of unbridled joy, so potent it made his eyes sting. A fleeting image accompanied it: a small child, mouth open in a perfect 'O' of delight, catching the first, fat snowflake of winter on their tongue. The shimmer faded a second later, the feeling evaporating and leaving Arthur with a bittersweet emptiness.

He walked on, his senses stretched to their limits. The Glimmerwood was not just a place; it was a living archive, a sensory overload of poignant history. He passed a darker, purple-black shimmer that pulsed with the heavy, cloying feeling of a forgotten apology, the gut-wrenching weight of regret hanging in the air. Another, a soft, rosy pink haze, held the echo of a lullaby hummed by a voice saturated with love—a comfort he couldn't remember.

He wasn't just seeing these echoes; he was feeling them. His resonance, the part of him attuned to the quiet stories of objects, was here dialled to a deafening volume. He was a tuning fork in a room of bells, vibrating in sympathy with every emotional frequency.

He followed the quartz path as it curved beside a stream. The water was not merely clear; it was like flowing air, so transparent he could see every rounded stone on the bottom, each seeming to contain a captured, miniature galaxy of soft light. He knelt, cupping his hands and drinking. The water was so cold it made his teeth ache and his head ring, but it tasted of the purest, most forgotten concept of freshness—like the first water that had ever bubbled from the ground.

As he drank, the cold clarity washing through him, he noticed the first flaw in the paradise. A subtle wrongness. Just off the path, the vibrant, glowing moss was thin and sickly. In its place was a pale, leprous-looking fungus that gave off no light, only a faint, bitter odour of ozone and static—the smell of a television left on an empty channel. The air above this patch was colder, and the colorful shimmers of memory were absent. It was a void, a blank spot in the forest's vibrant tapestry.

A deep unease, the first since he'd stepped through the Threshold, began to stir. This was not just a place of beauty; it was a place under a subtle, creeping siege.

His thoughts were interrupted by a soft, rustling chitter. It was the first true, animal-like sound he'd heard, and it came from a thick tangle of glowing roots to his right. He froze, his heart leaping into his throat. Slowly, he turned.

Nestled in the crook of a great, moss-covered root was a small, intricate nest, woven from moss, dried leaves, and strands of what looked like solidified shadow. And in the nest, looking at him with wide, terrified eyes, was a creature.

It was about the size of a squirrel, but bore no resemblance to any animal Arthur had ever seen. Its form was fluid, unstable, a thing of smoke and suggestion. One moment it seemed like a fox kit made of parchment, the next it shifted, and he saw the suggestion of a boy's face, formed from shifting patterns of leaf-shadow and old, whispered secrets. Its body flickered, a silent film projected on smoke. It was clutching a small, dull, and cracked river stone to its chest, shivering violently.

An Echo-Folk. The term surfaced in Arthur's mind from nowhere, a piece of instinctive knowledge granted by the Key. This was a native, a being woven from the very stuff of this place.

"Hello?" Arthur said, his voice a hushed, clumsy intrusion in the holy quiet. He winced.

The creature flinched, pressing itself deeper into the nest. It let out another sound, not a squeak or a growl, but a soft, rustling sigh, like pages turning in an empty library. The sound was full of fear.

Arthur knew that feeling intimately. He knelt, careful to keep his distance, to make himself small and non-threatening. He was an intruder here. He had to show he wasn't one of the Loud Ones. He was a collector. A listener.

Slowly, he reached into his pocket and pulled out his own smooth, grey stone—the most precious quiet thing he possessed. It was an anchor to his old world. He held it out on his flat hand, an offering.

"It's okay," he whispered, pouring all the gentleness he possessed into his voice. "I'm not going to hurt you. I'm just… visiting."

The creature's large, luminous eyes, like pools of liquid amber, flickered from Arthur's face to the stone. Its shivering stilled. It uncurled slightly, and one flickering, half-substantial paw reached out from the nest. It wasn't reaching for Arthur's stone, but pointing, trembling, past him, deeper into the woods.

Arthur followed its gesture. There, between the grand, ancient trees, the air was different. The colourful shimmers of memory were fewer and farther between. The spaces were darker, emptier. The very light seemed thinner, drained of its magic, tinged with the same grey static he'd sensed from the sickly moss. The air that drifted from that direction was cold in a way that had nothing to do with temperature. It was the cold of absence. The cold of a blank page where a story should be. It was the feeling of the Great Amnesia, a term that also surfaced in his mind, full of dreadful finality.

A sudden, sharp crack echoed through the wood—twisted, wrong, as if the sound itself was being unmade. It didn't echo; it was swallowed by the profound silence that followed.

The little Echo-Folk let out a terrified rustle and vanished, its form dissolving into the shadows of the root as if it had never been there.

Arthur scrambled to his feet, his heart hammering against his ribs. He was no longer alone. Down the path, in the direction of the spreading emptiness, a figure stood.

It was tall and impossibly thin, a man-shaped void in the fabric of the forest. It didn't block the light; it was a place where light ceased to exist. Its surface was a shifting static, the grey snow of a dead television channel, and it seemed to pull the very sound from the air around it, creating a pocket of profound, deafening silence. It had no face, but Arthur could feel its attention on him—a passive, indifferent regard that was more frightening than any hatred.

The Alchemist of Absence had found him.

It took a step forward. It made no sound. The vibrant, glowing moss at its feet didn't bend or crush; it simply greyed and turned to dust, its light extinguished forever.

Arthur stumbled backward, his breath catching in his throat. The thing was between him and the path back to the doorway. He was trapped in this beautiful, dying world, with the embodiment of nothingness gliding silently toward him.

CHAPTER FOUR

THE FIRST ERRAND

Fear, Arthur discovered, was a loud, hot, and messy thing. It shouted in his blood, hammered in his ears, and turned his limbs to water. But the fear the Alchemist inspired was of a different, more terrifying order. It was cold. It was a silencing. The frantic, internal scream of his own panic felt profane and useless in the face of this advancing void, like trying to extinguish a star with a shout. His instinct to run, to make any noise at all, was smothered under a blanket of absolute stillness.

The Alchemist took another soundless step. The hem of Arthur's pajama pants, which had brushed against a vibrant, blue-leafed fern, suddenly felt coarse and grey. He looked down to see the color draining from the flannel, the memory of the dye, the very concept of "blue," being unmade. The threads themselves seemed to fray at the edges, not with age, but with non-existence.

That small, personal loss, the erasure of something so intimately his, broke the spell of cosmic terror. A raw, primal instinct took over:

Run.

He did not run *from* the path, but along it, deeper into the Glimmerwood, away from the Alchemist and the shimmering promise of the doorway home. The pale quartz path was his only guide, a thread of familiarity in the increasingly bewildering landscape. He risked a frantic glance over his shoulder. The Alchemist did not quicken its pace. It simply glided, an eraser moving over a drawing, its progress inevitable and unhurried. It was not chasing him; it was merely... continuing. And its path would eventually intersect with his.

The forest began to change as he fled. The gentle, joyful shimmers of memory became fewer, replaced by darker, more frantic echoes. He passed a shimmer of deep crimson that pulsed with the feeling of a last, desperate goodbye—a ghost of a hand slipping from another, the finality of a closing door, the weight of words forever unspoken. He flinched away, the emotion so sharp and personal it felt like a cut to his own soul.

Further on, a swirling, sickly green echo emitted waves of gnawing envy, so potent Arthur felt a brief, irrational resentment toward the rooted, certain lives of the trees themselves. The very sound of the forest was thinning. The melodic trickle of the stream had faded somewhere behind him, and the wind now hissed through bare, silver branches like a serpent, carrying a fine, grey dust that coated his tongue with the taste of ashes and forgetting.

He was running out of world. The vibrant, bioluminescent life was receding, replaced by skeletal remains. The quartz path beneath his feet began to feel less substantial, the crystals grinding into a dull powder.

His lungs burned. He stumbled over a root that had turned brittle as charcoal, crumbling to dust at his touch. He fell hard, his hands scraping against the disintegrating path. Pushing himself up, panting, he saw it. A dead end. Not a wall, but something worse. The path simply stopped, and beyond it was… nothing. A grey, featureless expanse. It was not a fog or darkness; it was a lack. It was the non-place the Alchemist created, and it was spreading, swallowing the Glimmerwood bite by bite. He was trapped in the final, shrinking corner.

The void was ahead. The Alchemist was behind.

Despair, colder than the air, more absolute than the void, gripped him. He was just a boy with a pocket full of stones. He pulled his knees to his chest, the Key digging into his leg, a mocking reminder of the wonder that had led him to this end. He had been a fool to think he was anything more than a momentary curiosity, soon to be erased like everything else.

A sound. Not the Alchemist's silence, but a real sound. A soft, frantic chittering.

He looked up, tears of frustration and fear blurring his vision. There, on a low-hanging branch just to his left, was the small Echo-Folk. It was flickering wildly, its form shifting from fox, to boy, to a tangle of knotted light. It was gesturing wildly, not at the path, but at the solid-looking wall of thorns and twisted, black-barked tree trunks to his right.

"There's no way through," Arthur whispered, his voice thick with defeat.

The creature chittered again, a sound of immense frustration. It leaped from the branch and scurried to the wall of vegetation, and, before Arthur's eyes, simply stepped into it. Its form dissolved, merging with the shadows between the thorns. A moment later, its head—looking like that of a worried, shadowy squirrel—poked back out. It gestured with urgent, choppy motions for him to follow.

It was impossible. The thorns were as long as his fingers, needle-sharp and gleaming with a dark, oily light. He risked another glance back. The Alchemist was closer now, maybe fifty yards away, a silent, gliding doom. The air around it was dead. The beautiful, sad shimmers along the path were winking out one by one as it passed, like stars being blotted out by a cloud.

He had no choice.

Trusting the creature, Arthur pushed himself to his feet and ran toward the wall. As he got closer, he saw it. A secret path, so narrow it was almost invisible, hidden behind a curtain of weeping willow-like branches that were not green, but the color of tarnished silver. It was an opening just wide enough for a boy to squeeze through.

He plunged into the gap, the silvery leaves brushing his face like cold, metallic fingers. He forced his way through, thorns tugging and snagging his jacket. For a terrifying moment, he was stuck, wedged between two unyielding trunks, the Alchemist's chilling presence drawing nearer. He could feel the temperature dropping, the silence pressing in from behind. With a final, desperate heave, he popped through, stumbling forward into a hidden clearing.

He turned back, chest heaving. The Alchemist had reached the end of the path. It stood at the wall of thorns, its featureless head seeming to regard the hidden opening. It raised a hand of static. The silver leaves at the edge of the path began to curl, grey, and dissolve into motes of dust. It was going to unmake the secret path.

But then, it stopped. It lowered its hand. As if deciding this particular corner, this one hidden boy, was not a priority in its vast, entropic agenda, it simply turned and glided back the way it had come, continuing its slow, methodical consumption of the main path.

Arthur sank to his knees in the soft, glowing moss, gasping with profound relief. He was safe. For now.

As his breathing slowed, he took in his surroundings. This clearing was different from the rest of the wood. It was a perfect circle, sheltered by a domed canopy of interwoven golden branches that hummed with a low, protective energy. In the center stood a single, magnificent tree, its bark the color of moonlight, its leaves like delicate shavings of opal that refracted the soft light into tiny, dancing rainbows. This was a place of power. A sanctuary.

And nestled amidst its roots was a collection of things that looked wildly out of place. A chipped teacup with a faded floral pattern sat beside a tarnished silver locket. A child's wooden boat rested near a single, worn-out leather boot. A cracked pottery bowl, a glass marble, a pair of broken spectacles mended with wire. It was a tiny, fragile ecosystem of lost things, a museum of the mundane and the mourned.

The Echo-Folk was there, watching him from atop a stack of weathered, titleless books. Its form had stabilized slightly, now mostly resembling a small, slender boy woven from walnut shells and deep brown shadows. It was still clutching the cracked river stone, like a talisman.

"You… you saved me," Arthur said, his voice barely a whisper, filled with a reverence he'd never felt.

The creature tilted its head. It did not speak, but a series of images and feelings appeared in Arthur's mind, flowing into him like water. You are Resonant. You feel the echoes. You are not like the others. The Loud Ones.

"The Loud Ones?"

An image of his own world flashed in his mind—blurry, rushed, filled with glaring lights and people who never stopped to listen to the hum of a stone. He saw the frantic energy of the school hallway, the distracted gaze of his parents.

"You mean… my people," Arthur said, understanding dawning. He was different, even among his own kind. His resonance wasn't a flaw; it was a key in itself.

The creature nodded its shimmering head. It gestured to the collection of objects around the tree. A wave of profound sadness and fierce, protective love washed over Arthur. These are the Last Things. The ones almost forgotten. I am their keeper. I am Fig.

"Fig," Arthur repeated. The name felt right. Simple and solid, like the stone in his own pocket.

Fig pointed a delicate, twig-like finger at Arthur's pocket, from which the Key still emanated a soft, warm hum. Arthur reached in and pulled out the heavy, dark key.

A new feeling from Fig, one of immense age and weary recognition. The Key. It has been lost. The Threshold has been closed.

"The threshold? You mean the doorway?"

Fig nodded, a grave expression on its faintly defined face. The Glimmerwood has been cut off. The Loud Ones forget. They do not listen. The Amnesia grows. The Alchemist consumes. A final, desperate feeling accompanied by an image of the magnificent moon-barked tree. The Heartwood is failing. When it goes silent, all of this…

The feeling that followed was the most terrifying of all. It wasn't an image of destruction or fire. It was a feeling of… nothing. A gentle, final, quiet end. Not a bang, but a whimper that stretched into eternity.

Arthur looked from the Key in his hand to Fig's large, luminous eyes, filled with the weight of centuries of loss. He looked at the chipped teacup, the lonely boot, the Heartwood with its faint, almost invisible cracks. He was not just a visitor. He hadn't just found a secret world.

He had arrived at the scene of a slow, silent, cosmic death. And he, Arthur Pensive, the boy who collected subtle truths, was the only one who could hear its dying breath.

CHAPTER FIVE

THE SYMPHONY OF ALMOST-LOST

The silence in the clearing was not the dead silence of the Ashen Wastes, but a reverent quiet, like that of a cathedral between hymns. It held space for the fragile stories contained in the chipped teacup, the lonely boot, the faded locket. Arthur sat with his back against the Heartwood, the tree's strange, warm vibration seeping into his bones, a stark contrast to the cold dread that had taken root in his stomach. Fig had saved him, but from what? An ending so vast and final he could barely comprehend it.

Fig moved around the clearing with a new, grim purpose. The creature's earlier skittishness had been burned away, replaced by a solemn, focused energy. It was no longer just a keeper; it was a soldier preparing its charges for a war of existence. Arthur watched as it scurried from object to object, its form flickering as it gently touched the wooden boat, or softly stroked the cracked pottery bowl. With each action, a faint, feeble echo of memory rose—like watching someone perform CPR on a dying patient.

I reinforce them, Fig's thought-voice came, strained and thin. *But my song is weak. There are too many. And I am... alone.*

The loneliness in that thought was a vast, cold ocean. Arthur felt it wash over him, so profound it made his own solitude seem a minor inconvenience. The weight of that unimaginable time—the last librarian in a world that was forgetting—was heavy.

"What can I do?" Arthur asked, his voice feeling too loud for this delicate space. "You said I'm Resonant. What does that mean?"

Fig turned its luminous eyes to him. It padded closer and, hesitantly, reached out a hand that looked like woven birch bark, pointing not at an object, but at Arthur's own chest.

You do not just feel the echoes. You can... answer them.

Fig's meaning unfolded in Arthur's mind like a complex origami: a concept of harmonic resonance. When a memory shimmered, it emitted a specific emotional frequency. Arthur, as a Resonant, could hum that frequency back. He could, in a small way, reaffirm the memory's existence, its right to be. He could sing its song back, strengthening its signal against the relentless, silent static of the Amnesia. It wasn't about creation; it was about bearing witness, about declaring: *I hear you. You matter.*

"Show me," Arthur said, determination hardening his

voice. He couldn't fight the Alchemist directly, but this felt right. This was a deeper, more active form of listening.

Fig led him to the tarnished silver locket. It lay cold and inert on a bed of velvety moss. As Fig placed a twig-finger on it, a weak, grey shimmer rose, carrying a feeling of profound, aching loss. The image of a young woman staring out a rain-streaked window flickered for a nanosecond before dissolving.

She waited by a window, Fig communicated, the thought heavy with the dust of centuries. *He never came back from the sea. The story is almost gone.*

Arthur knelt. He closed his eyes, blocking out everything but the feeling emanating from the locket. It was the specific sadness of hope deferred, day after day, until it crumbled into a fine, grey dust of acceptance—an echo of a love that had become a monument to absence.

He let the quiet, ancient grief fill him. He found its shape, its weight, its texture in his soul. And then, from that same deep place from which his empathy had always flowed, he began to hum.

It wasn't a melody he knew. It was a low, steady, minor-key note that vibrated in his throat and chest, a sound that felt the way the memory did. It was an act of empathy so pure it was physically draining. He felt a part of his own attention flowing out of him and into the shimmer.

As he hummed, the grey shimmer brightened, shifting to a soft, silvery light. The feeling of loss was still there, but it was no longer desolate. It was… honored. Remembered. The locket itself seemed to warm slightly under Fig's touch, and the tarnish lessened, a few specks of its original brilliance winking back into existence.

He stopped, the note dying in his throat, and opened his eyes. A wave of exhaustion washed over him. He felt lighter, yet also more connected, more solid.

Fig was staring, its large eyes wide with something like awe. A feeling of profound, earth-shattering hope bloomed in Arthur's mind. *You see?* Fig's thought was a whisper of pure wonder. *You are not just a visitor. You are a Restorer.*

The word hung in the air, immense and terrifying. A Restorer. It was the opposite of everything he felt in his own life, where he was powerless, overlooked. Here, his quietness was not a weakness; it was a tool. His sensitivity was not a flaw; it was a force.

"But this is just one locket," Arthur said, his voice hoarse. "The Alchemist is out there, erasing whole paths. It's… it's endless."

Fig's hopeful expression dimmed. It looked toward the opal-leaved Heartwood. As Arthur looked closer, he saw the hairline cracks running through its moon-pale bark—signs of sickness.

The Heartwood is the source, Fig explained. *It is the anchor. It is sick because the world forgets. The small echoes we reinforce here are like… bandages. To heal it, we must find and restore the source of the sickness. We must find and bring back the Lost Cores.*

"Lost Cores?" The term felt heavy, foundational.

Images flooded Arthur's mind, more vivid than any before. He saw:

- A single, perfect, crystalline musical note—the final, unresolved note of a symphony whose composer had died before its completion.
- The true, secret name of a star—a word of power whispered only once, now lost to astronomy.
- The scent of a forgotten flower—a fragrance that could cure despair, its last petal crumbled to dust.
- The feeling of the very first act of kindness—the spark that started the chain of empathy.

These are not just memories, Fig explained. *They are foundational. They are the pillars that hold up the sky of our world. The Alchemist seeks them most of all. We must find them first. Your resonance can call them. My knowledge can guide us.*

A map, not of paper, but of feeling and image, laid itself out: a journey to the farthest, most damaged corners of the Glimmerwood. To the Mists of Unheard Melodies, to the Shore of Vanished Names, to the crumbling Archives of Fallen Kingdoms.

It was an impossible quest. He had school on Monday. He had parents who might not even notice he was gone. The sheer, terrifying scale of it made him want to curl up and hide.

He thought of the locket, and the woman who waited, and how her story now felt a little less lonely because he had restored it. He thought of his own pocket, full of quiet, ordinary things. Perhaps they were not so unimportant after all. Perhaps his entire life had been a training ground for this.

He stood up, his legs shaky but his resolve firm. "Which one do we save first?"

A feeling of fierce, blazing pride came from Fig. It returned holding something small and metallic that glinted: a single, tarnished trumpet valve.

The first Core is the most fragile, Fig's thought came, layered with the ghost of an unfinished symphony. *The Last Note of the Unfinished Symphony. Without it, all music will one day feel... incomplete. It lies in the Mists of Unheard Melodies, where the Alchemist's power is strong.*

Fig held out the valve. Arthur took it. As his fingers closed around the cold brass, a faint, desperate, and heartbreakingly beautiful strain of music teased the very edge of his hearing—a melody that begged to be resolved, a question that demanded an answer.

The quest had begun.

CHAPTER SIX

THE MISTS OF UNHEARD MELODIES

The journey out of the sanctuary felt like stepping from a warm, lit chapel into a cold, uncertain night. The vibrant, protective hum of the Heartwood's clearing faded with each step, replaced by the thinner, more sorrowful air of the main Glimmerwood. Arthur carried the trumpet valve in his pocket, its cold brass a constant, sobering reminder of the task ahead—a shard of a broken star, precious and dangerously fragile.

Fig led the way, its form a shifting beacon of walnut-brown and moss-green. Gone was the darting, nervous energy; in its place was a grim, tactical precision. It moved like a scout behind enemy lines, pausing often to press an ear-like swirl of bark against a tree trunk, listening to vibrations Arthur could not perceive.

The Amnesia feeds on pathways, Fig's thought-voice whispered, tight with focused urgency. *It follows the well-worn routes of memory first, the stories told and retold until they grow thin. We must travel the forgotten ways. The spaces between the stories.*

They left the comforting, pale quartz path behind, plunging into the deeper woods where the trees knitted together into a shadowy canopy, blocking out the soft glow. Arthur's world narrowed to Fig's flickering form and the weight of the Key in his opposite pocket, a solid, warm tether to safety.

The forest here was older and more sorrowful. The memories they passed were not clear, poignant shimmers, but twisted, dissonant things. A patch of air writhed in a silent, screeching cacophony—the echo of a furious argument, leaving only the raw, ugly emotion to poison the air. Another shimmer was a stagnant, muddy brown, heavy with the feeling of a brilliant idea that had vanished an instant before it could be grasped. Arthur felt a headache building, a pressure from all the unresolved, broken echoes. It was like walking through a hospital for feelings, where every patient was terminally ill with forgetting.

After what felt like an hour, the light began to change. The gold and violet hues of the Glimmerwood faded, bleached away as if by a milky fog. The air grew thick and damp, and a new sound emerged—a constant, low, mournful hum, like a cello string bowed by a ghost. It was the collective sound of every melody left unfinished, every song interrupted, every symphony abandoned mid-crescendo. The sound of artistic death.

They had reached the Mists of Unheard Melodies.

The mist itself was not made of water, but of something

finer and more sorrowful. It swirled around their ankles in lazy, sound-absorbing coils, muffling their footsteps. Shapes formed and dissolved within it: the ghost of a violin with broken strings, a shimmering piano key that melted before it could be struck, a ribbon of sheet music that unraveled into meaningless notes.

Stay close, Fig's thought was sharp with warning. *The mists can confuse. They make you hear... possibilities. They reflect your own desire back at you.*

As if on cue, a breathtakingly beautiful strain of music wafted past Arthur's ear—a soaring, triumphant theme, the perfect, golden resolution to the unfinished phrase he'd heard from the valve. His heart leaped. The answer was right here! He took an impulsive step toward the sound.

No! Fig's mental cry was like a shove. A sharp, painful image of a fly lured into a spider's web flashed in his mind. *It is a lure. An echo of what you want to hear. The true Note does not call. It hides. It is too fragile to call attention to itself.*

Arthur shook his head, the beautiful music fading and leaving a hollow, aching void. The mist was treacherous. It preyed on hope itself.

They pressed on, deeper into the swirling, sound-drowned landscape. The ground became soft and spongy, littered with the ghostly impressions of instruments. The mournful hum was everywhere, a physical pressure seeping into his bones. He found himself fighting a deep, creeping despair. How could one small note matter against this crushing weight of forgotten sadness?

He tightened his grip on the valve. In response, a single, clear, and terribly lonely note pulsed from it—a pure, high C that cut through the oppressive hum for a single, brilliant second. It was a cry for help. A beacon of truth in a sea of lies.

Fig froze, its head cocked. *There. It answers you. It knows you are near. But so does the other.*

A different music began to weave through the mists. This one was not beautiful, but empty. It was a hollow, rhythmic knocking, like a dead branch tapping on a windowpane in a mindless pattern. It was the sound of silence pretending to be sound. The anti-music. And it was getting closer.

Through the mist, a tall, thin shape began to form.

The Alchemist.

It was here, drawn by the pure, potent pulse of the Lost Core. It moved through the mists, and where its static-filled form passed, the mournful hum wasn't just stopped; it was erased, replaced by a vacuum of absolute quiet. The ghostly instruments on the ground dissolved into grey dust.

Fig let out a terrified rustle. *It knows we are here for the Core! It will consume the Note before we can reach it!*

The hollow knocking sound intensified, a percussive void that smothered the fragile, crystalline resonance from the trumpet valve. Arthur felt the connection sever, the high C snuffed out like a candle. He was blind in the mist again, the true signal lost beneath the Alchemist's silencing static.

"What do we do?" he whispered, panic clawing at his

throat, his resolve crumbling.

Fig's large eyes darted from the advancing Alchemist to Arthur. A new feeling, one of desperate, wild strategy, emanated from the creature. *It is made of silence. It cannot tolerate true, willing sound. Not the echoes of the past... but a new sound. A loud one. A sound born of present feeling.*

"A loud one?" Arthur said, horrified. The idea of being loud here, in this sacred place of sorrow, felt like a sacrilege. It was everything he had always run from.

It is the only way! You must create a resonance it cannot erase! A sound so full of present, raw feeling it becomes a shield! You must sing, Arthur. Not an echo. Your own song!

The Alchemist was twenty yards away. The deadening silence around it was spreading, a bubble of nothingness that was consuming the mists. Arthur could feel his own thoughts starting to slow, to grey. The memory of his own name felt slippery, its edges fraying.

He looked at the terrified Fig. He thought of the woman with the locket, the unfinished symphony—all the unseen details that deserved to be remembered. He closed his eyes. He ignored the knocking, the creeping silence, the cold dread. He reached down, past the fear, and found the feeling of connection he had when he hummed to the locket. He gathered up every bit of wonder, fear, and fierce, protective love he felt for this strange world, and poured it all into his lungs.

And then Arthur Pensive, the quiet boy, sang.

It was not a word. It was a single, open-throated, resonant

note. It was his melody. The sound tore through the dead air, a golden, vibrant, living wave of pure feeling. It was clumsy. It was human. It was defiantly, beautifully alive.

The effect was instantaneous.

The Alchemist recoiled as if struck by a physical force. The static of its form rippled violently, patterns scrambling in confusion. The hollow, knocking rhythm stuttered and fell into disarray. It could not process this new, living sound. It was an anomaly in its universe of silence, a fire in its world of ice. For a few precious seconds, the Alchemist was stunned, its absolute focus shattered by spontaneous, heartfelt noise.

Now! Fig's thought was a triumphant spark. *Follow the true resonance!*

Freed from the Alchemist's smothering influence, the trumpet valve in Arthur's hand blazed with sudden warmth. The pure, high C sang out again, clear, strong, and desperate— a brilliant, unwavering thread of sound leading off to the left.

Still holding his own note, his voice growing hoarse, Arthur plunged after it, Fig scrambling at his heels. They dodged through the confused, swirling mists, following the clarion call of the Lost Core, leaving the stunned and baffled Alchemist in their wake.

They ran until Arthur's breath gave out and his song ended in a ragged gasp. They collapsed, panting, behind the crumbling ruins of a stone archway. The mist was thinner here. The oppressive hum had receded. And there, hovering in the center of the archway, pulsing with a soft, desperate light, was a single, shimmering, crystalline note.

It was the most beautiful and heartbreaking thing Arthur had ever seen. It hung in the air, a teardrop of solidified sound, and the air around it vibrated with the unfulfilled promise of a melody that would never, ever be complete.

They had found it.

CHAPTER SEVEN

THE WEIGHT OF A NOTE

The moment Arthur's own defiant song ended, the Mists of Unheard Melodies rushed back in, not with their previous mournful hum, but with a new, sharper tone— a dissonant, jealous rage. The crystalline note, the Last Note of the Unfinished Symphony, hung in the air before them, a teardrop of solidified sound pulsing with a fragile, terrified light. It was the heart of this entire region, and they had laid hands upon its sanctuary.

Fig was already on its feet, its form pulled taut with urgency, its large eyes scanning the swirling mists. *It is fragile. More than glass. A thought of doubt could shatter it. And the Alchemist will not be distracted for long. Your song was a stone in its path. It has already stepped around it.*

As if summoned by the thought, the deadening silence began to seep back into the edges of their small haven. The hollow, rhythmic knocking was distant, a persistent, metronomic counterpoint to the Note's pure frequency. It was getting closer, more focused. The Alchemist was re-orienting itself, its singular, entropic purpose renewed and now sharpened with chilling focus: them.

"How do we carry it?" Arthur whispered, afraid that even his ragged breath might disturb the Core's delicate equilibrium. It wasn't a physical object. It was a concept given form. How did one transport an ending that refused to end?

Fig's thought was a swift, practical stream, a stark contrast to the artistic tragedy before them. *It cannot be touched by hands, which are made for forgetting. It must be carried in a vessel of resonance. A thing that remembers music.*

Arthur's mind raced. He looked down at the trumpet valve in his hand, the object that had led them here. It was cold brass, but it had potential. It had been kissed by breath and vibration. He held it out towards the hovering note.

"Will this work?"

Fig considered it, probing the valve with its resonance. *It is a part... but it is not whole. Its memory is weak. It may not be strong enough to hold the Core's entire truth. The Note's sorrow is... immense.*

The knocking was louder now, a fist hammering against the door of perception. The mist behind them was thinning, bleached to a pale, uniform grey. They were out of time. Arthur could feel the static prickle on the back of his neck, the air growing thin and cold.

"It's all we have," Arthur said, his voice tight with a fear that was no longer for himself, but for this precious, impossible thing.

He took a step forward, the valve held cupped in both hands like a priest holding a sacred relic. As he approached, the crystalline note pulsed, and the strain of the unfinished melody filled his mind, so poignant and beautiful it felt like a physical wound. He saw the ghost of a grand orchestra, frozen mid-crescendo, the conductor's baton poised for the downbeat that never came. The sorrow was a tidal wave.

Slowly, carefully, he raised the valve until it was directly beneath the hovering note.

"Please," he breathed, directing the plea at the Note, the Glimmerwood, the universe itself.

For a terrifying second, nothing happened. The Note continued to pulse, separate, untouchable. Despair, colder than the Alchemist's silence, began to grip his heart.

Then, as if recognizing a fragment of its own origin, the note descended. It settled, merging with the cold brass like light being absorbed by a prism. The valve glowed with a soft, internal light, and the metal grew warm in Arthur's palms. The unfinished melody was now a constant, quiet hum, a secret he held—a burden and a promise. The vessel held.

You have it! Fig's thought was a burst of exhilaration. *Now, we must run! The Alchemist will be enraged!*

The world reacted the moment the Note was contained. The mournful hum of the mists sharpened into a wail of protest. The hollow knocking of the Alchemist became a frantic, furious pounding, the sound of logic and silence defied.

They burst from behind the stone archway just as the Alchemist emerged from the mist. The passive indifference was gone. Its static form crackled with aggressive energy, the grey snow churning like a storm cloud. The void around it was now reaching, stretching out tendrils of nothingness, actively seeking to unmake.

Arthur clutched the glowing valve to his chest, the heat seeping through his jacket, and ran. Fig was a blur ahead of him, leading them on a desperate, direct route back towards the Heartwood's clearing. It was a race against erasure. Branches, once beautiful, seemed to whip at his face with malevolent intent. The Glimmerwood itself, in its corrupted state, seemed to resist their escape.

He risked a glance back. The Alchemist was gliding after them, faster than before. The tendrils of silence lashed out, and a vibrant, blue-flowered bush that shimmered with the memory of a first kiss simply vanished, replaced by a patch of grey, featureless earth. It wasn't just being destroyed; it was being retroactively negated.

Do not look back! Fig's command was a mental scream. *It feeds on attention! Its nature is to be the only thing that is!*

Arthur focused ahead, his legs burning. The weight of the note in his hands was not physical, but a weight of responsibility. He was carrying a piece of the world's soul. Its warmth was the warmth of a dying star, and he was its last custodian.

They broke out of the twisted, angry trees and back onto the main quartz path. The familiar, pale road was a relief, but the Alchemist was close, its silence swallowing the sound of their footfalls, the path's vibrant colours leaching to grey in its wake.

"Fig, it's too fast!" Arthur cried, his breath coming in ragged, burning gasps. He could feel the static now, a greasy sensation on his skin, the precursor to unbeing.

Fig skidded to a halt, turning to face the pursuing void. *The Glimmerwood is more than memories. It is also protection. It can still fight for itself.*

Fig raised its twig-like hands and began to hum, not a melody, but a low, resonant, fundamental note—the sound of roots digging deep, of bark growing thick, of time itself piling up in layers of stubborn existence. In response, the ancient trees lining the path groaned with immense, waking power. Their branches, heavy with glowing leaves, began to weave together into a thick, living, pulsating wall between the children and the Alchemist.

It was not a permanent barrier. As the Alchemist reached the wall, the static touch began to grey the leaves and turn the wood brittle. But it was slow. For the first time, the Alchemist had to work to erase something. The ancient wall, invested with millennia of will, bought them precious seconds.

Go! Fig's thought was strained. *To the clearing! I cannot hold this for long!*

Arthur turned and sprinted, the glowing valve held tight

against his hammering heart. He didn't stop until he saw the familiar, hidden entrance behind the silver willow branches. He plunged through, stumbling into the safe, silent clearing, and collapsed at the base of the magnificent Heartwood tree, wracked with exhaustion and relief.

He lay there, gasping, the world spinning. A moment later, Fig tumbled through the opening after him, its light dimmed to a faint ember. The creature was utterly spent.

But they had done it.

Slowly, shakily, Arthur pushed himself to his knees. He looked down at the valve, pulsing gently with the captured light of the Last Note.

Holding his breath, as if approaching a sleeping god, he placed the valve gently against the tree's moon-pale bark.

The effect was immediate and glorious.

A wave of pure, golden sound—the completed, resolved phrase of the symphony—rippled out from the point of contact. It was a profound vibration that passed through Arthur, through Fig, through the very air of the clearing. The cracks in the bark nearest the valve sealed themselves, smooth as new skin, the color returning to a vibrant, healthy silver. The opal leaves above shimmered, their light intensifying, casting dancing, rainbow-hued shadows.

A feeling of profound, cosmic relief flooded the clearing. One foundational piece of the universe had been slotted back into place. The air itself seemed easier to breathe.

Arthur sat back, awe-struck. He had done that. He and Fig. He, Arthur Pensive, had restored a part of creation.

But the triumph was short-lived. Fig was looking not at the healed portion of the tree, but at the rest of it, where the sickness still held sway. The Alchemist was still out there, wounded but not defeated. And they had two more Cores to find.

The first battle was won. But the war for the very existence of wonder had just begun.

CHAPTER EIGHT

THE COST OF FORGETTING

The triumph in the clearing was as fragile as the crystalline Note had been. It lasted only as long as the echo of the completed symphony hung in the air, a golden afterglow that slowly faded into the Glimmerwood's perpetual twilight. As the final, resolved chord dissolved, the sorrowful hum of the forest returned, and with it, the grim reality of their task.

Fig did not rest. While Arthur sat with his back against the Heartwood, the little Echo-Folk moved with a grim, focused speed, weaving a single, shimmering strand of light—a distilled essence of memory—into its own flickering form.

The Alchemist is angered, Fig's thought-voice came, sharp and clear. It felt us restore the Note. It felt the Balance shift. It will not be tricked again by simple noise. We must be subtle, Arthur. We must be unseen.

Arthur pushed himself to his feet, his body a landscape of aches. "Which Core is next? And what is the challenge now?"

Fig paused by a small, weathered piece of driftwood, bleached white by a sun that no longer existed in this realm. It placed a delicate hand on the wood, and a feeling of vast, empty spaces and profound identity loss washed over Arthur.

The True Name of the First Star, Fig communicated, the thought heavy with the gravity of a lost constellation. The word whispered to call it into being from the primordial dark. Without it, all names lose a little of their power. All things become a little less themselves.

An image formed in Arthur's mind: a shore of black, volcanic sand under a sky the color of a day-old bruise. In that sky was a single, gaping hole where a brilliant constellation should have been.

That is the Shore of Vanished Names. It is a place the Alchemist has almost wholly consumed. Its silence is not merely a field there; it is the very ground we walk upon. It is the very nature of the place.

"How do we find a Name in a field of silence?" Arthur asked, the cold dread returning.

The Name, Fig explained, will not be a sound. It will be a pattern. A vibration in the sand, a shape repeating in the silence. You will have to use your resonance to listen, not for noise, but for structure. You must find a single, specific vibration in a universe of static.

The plan, as Fig laid it out in a complex rush of images,

was less a battle and more a delicate infiltration. They would cross the Ashen Wastes, a grey, skeletal landscape. When they reached the Shore, Arthur would have to open his resonance to the deafening vacuum and become nothing but a point of pure observation.

But the Alchemist will be waiting, Fig's confirmation was grim. It is a sentinel there. It will feel your resonance probing the silence.

Arthur felt a flicker of deep-seated fear. The last time, they had shouted to escape. This time, they couldn't even think too loudly.

Fig placed a small, twig-like hand on Arthur's arm. This is my role. While you face the pattern, I will draw the Alchemist's attention by becoming an anti-void. I will become a complex target. I will make myself a moving library of stories, too multifaceted for the Alchemist to simplify quickly. It will demand its entire, analytic focus to deconstruct.

"It will erase you," Arthur protested, the memory of Fig's close call still painful.

I am not the same as I was. You have shared your resonance with me, Arthur. I am Fig, your friend. And I will not let you face this alone. I will be the most unforgettable thing in the entire Wastes.

The resolve in those thoughts was unshakeable. Arthur was the scalpel, tasked with a delicate, precise operation. Fig was the shield, woven from memory, who would draw the blade.

They prepared with a solemn intensity. Arthur focused on the smooth stone in his pocket, allowing the despair he would inevitably feel on the Shore to pass through him without drowning him. He had to become a pure void himself, but a void that listened.

When the time came, they stood together at the edge of the clearing. The path to the Shore beyond was a road of black, polished stone that swallowed the light—a road of endings.

For the Glimmerwood, Fig thought.

For the Quiet Things, Arthur replied in his own mind.

Together, they stepped onto the black road and began the long, dark journey, their fates more intertwined than ever before.

CHAPTER NINE

THE SHORE OF VANISHED NAMES

The journey out of the Glimmerwood's heartland was a descent. With each step on the black, light-swallowing road, the vibrant, melancholic beauty of the forest fell away, replaced by a creeping greyness that felt less like a colour and more like the absence of all others. The air grew thin and cold, carrying a fine, abrasive dust that coated Arthur's tongue with the taste of ozone and forgotten words. The comforting, sorrowful hum of memories was abruptly snipped off. This new silence was not the living quiet of the Glimmerwood's sanctuary, but a dead, hollow thing—the silence of a vacuum, of a mouth open in a scream that has long since lost its voice.

This was the Ashen Wastes. The trees here were petrified, their forms twisted into agonized, silver-grey sculptures, their branches frozen in desperate gestures against a slate-coloured sky. There was no moss, no bioluminescence, no shimmering echoes. Only dust, stone, and a profound, chilling stillness. Arthur felt his own thoughts begin to slow, to simplify. The memory of his mother's face, the warmth of the Key—they all began to feel distant, abstract, like facts from a history book.

Fig moved beside him, a small, focused point of defiance in the overwhelming grey. Its cloak of memories glowed softly, a tiny, brave constellation in the expanse. Its communication was stripped down to the barest essentials, tactical images landing with the clarity of ice.

Danger. Close. The Amnesia is not a presence here; it is the ground we walk on. Do not think too loudly. Your own memories are anchors. Cling to them.

Arthur focused on the smooth stone in his pocket, on the golden chord of the completed symphony, on the feeling of Fig's trust. He built a small, quiet fortress in his mind, a constant effort, like holding his breath underwater.

Soon, the petrified forest gave way to a vast, open plain under a seamless sheet of bruised purple sky. In the center, where the horizon should have been, was the Shore of Vanished Names. It was an expanse of black, volcanic sand stretching out to meet a flat, grey nothingness. This wasn't water; it was the pure, unadulterated void, the raw material of the Alchemist's being. Directly overhead was a perfect, black circle, an absence so absolute it felt like a hole punched through reality itself.

But it was the Shore itself that was the true source of horror. It was littered with pale, wispy after-images—the ghosts of ghosts. A transparent, forgotten chair sat half-buried in the sand. The outline of an animal no one had ever named paced a silent, endless circle. They were unresolved equations, facts without context, waiting for the final erasure.

And walking among them was the Alchemist.

It was not hunting. It was tending. A gardener in a field of dying flowers. It moved slowly, and as it passed its static-filled form over the pale echoes, they would simply dissolve, their faint claim on existence gently, efficiently erased. There was no malice, only a passive, terrifyingly efficient purpose. It was a shepherd of oblivion.

Fig's small hand gripped Arthur's arm, an iron command to freeze. They crouched behind the skeletal trunk of a massive, fallen tree, watching. This was so much worse than the Mists. Here, the Alchemist was home.

The Name, Fig's thought was the barest whisper. It will not be a sound. It will be a pattern. A vibration in the sand, a shape repeating in the silence. Listen. Not with your ears. With your... you.

Arthur closed his eyes, reaching out with his resonance. At first, he felt nothing but the vast, hungry emptiness of the Amnesia, a suction pulling at his very sense of self. His own name began to feel thin, meaningless. He felt the memory of the grey stone soften at the edges. Panic, cold and sharp, lanced through him. He was dissolving.

Anchors, Fig's thought came, a lifeline. Your mother's voice. Your father's hand. The Key.

He clung to them, desperately. He focused on his mother singing a silly song, the warm weight of his father's hand, the solid hum of the Key.

And then, through the static, he felt it.

A tiny, rhythmic pulse, like a faint, struggling heartbeat under the black sand. It wasn't a sound, but a shape—a series of intricate, interlocking runes, a word of power, repeating over and over. It was fighting desperately not to be erased. It was coming from a spot frighteningly close to the Alchemist.

He opened his eyes and pointed, his hand trembling. Fig went rigid with a fear so profound it was a physical force. The Alchemist was drifting directly toward that spot, its passive erasure mere feet from where the Name pulsed its last, desperate rhythm.

There was no time for a plan, no time for a song, only a raw, unthinking reaction. As the Alchemist paused, Arthur's protective empathy shot out: a single, clear thought. It was not a shout. It was a command. A refusal so fundamental it was woven into the fabric of his being.

NO.

It was the same resonance he had used on the locket, amplified a thousandfold by desperation. It was a declaration of existence. This thing is. I bear witness. You shall not pass.

In the absolute silence of the Shore, the force of that single, resonant thought was like a physical shove. The Alchemist shuddered. It stopped. Its featureless head, a swirl of grey static, slowly turned from the spot on the sand.

And looked directly at them.

The void of its attention was a crushing pressure on Arthur's makeshift mental fortress. The Alchemist was now a predator poked with a stick. The static of its form churned, and it began to glide toward their hiding place, a wave of nothingness ready to break over them.

It sees us! Fig's thought was a raw blast of panic. It truly SEES us!

The Alchemist changed direction and advanced, the sphere of absolute silence now a weapon, actively seeking them. The air grew thin, the light dimming. Arthur felt a coldness seep into his bones—the cold of being forgotten before you were even gone.

"The Name!" Arthur gasped, his voice a pathetic, strangled thing. "It's going to erase it!"

Fig was paralyzed, a statue of terror.

But Arthur was a collector of unspoken stories. The quietest thing of all was a secret on the verge of being lost forever. He couldn't let it go. The pulse of the Name beneath the sand was a frantic, dying bird in his chest. He had to reach it.

He broke the spell of his own fear and scrambled out into the open, his movements clumsy and loud in the profound hush.

Arthur, NO! Fig's thought was a desperate, final plea.

The Alchemist was mere yards away now. Arthur could feel the static prickle on his skin, a sensation like a million tiny erasers rubbing him out. The memory of his breakfast vanished completely. The name of his street slipped from his mind, then returned, frayed and thin.

He fell to his knees at the pulse spot. He pressed his palms flat against the ground, ignoring the advancing void, and poured every ounce of his resonance into the sand.

I am here, he thought, shouting with his soul. I hear you. I remember you.

The pulse under his hands strengthened, a desperate, grateful rhythm. The interlocking runes of the True Name burned against his mind's eye. He knew them. He held them in his mind, a perfect, crystalline word.

A shadow fell over him.

He looked up. The Alchemist loomed, a tower of nothingness. It blotted out the bruised sky. It reached for him with a hand of static and silence, not in anger, but with the inevitable, gentle finality of an ending. This was it. He was going to be unmade.

Then, a flash of brown and green. Fig launched itself from behind the log, not at the Alchemist, but at Arthur. It placed its small, twig-like hands on Arthur's temples.

And it pushed.

It was a push of memory. A torrent of images and feelings—Arthur's own—flooded into him. It was a desperate, wild gamble to remind the silent thing of what it was trying to erase. Arthur saw his mother smiling as she taught him to tie his shoes, felt the warm weight of his father's hand after a nightmare. He remembered the joy of the snowflake, the sorrow of the locket, the triumphant beauty of the completed symphony. He was not a single memory to be erased, but a universe of them. Fig was reminding the Alchemist that Arthur was a library.

The Alchemist's hand stopped, an inch from Arthur's face. The static churned, confused. Its purpose was singular: find a thing that is, and make it not. But Arthur, in that moment, was everything. To unmake him would be to unmake a cosmos of echoes. The effort required was... illogical. Inefficient.

For a single, impossible second, the Alchemist hesitated.

It was the only chance they would get.

With the True Name burning in his mind, Arthur scrambled backward, grabbing the barely-conscious Fig, whose form was now faint and flickering.

And he ran.

He ran with the determined, solid strength of a keeper. He ran for the skeletal trees, for the path, for the Heartwood. He did not look back.

He heard no pursuit. The Alchemist did not follow. It simply stood on the Shore of Vanished Names, a monument to silence, perhaps still calculating the immense cost of extinguishing the boy who was suddenly, defiantly, so full of noise and life.

They had not defeated it. They had baffled it. And in doing

so, they had stolen the True Name of the First Star right from under its featureless nose.

Arthur ran until his lungs were fire. He collapsed in the relative safety of the stunted woods, Fig cradled weakly in his arms. The little Echo-Folk looked up at him, its eyes dim but full of respect.

You, Fig's thought was a faint, awed whisper, are more Resonant than I ever dreamed.

Arthur, breathing in ragged gasps, nodded. He focused on the brilliant, runic word held safe in his mind. He could feel its power, a tiny, restored anchor in the fabric of reality.

They had the second Core. But the cost of this victory was written in the faint, flickering form of his friend. The real battle, he realized with cold dread, was just beginning.

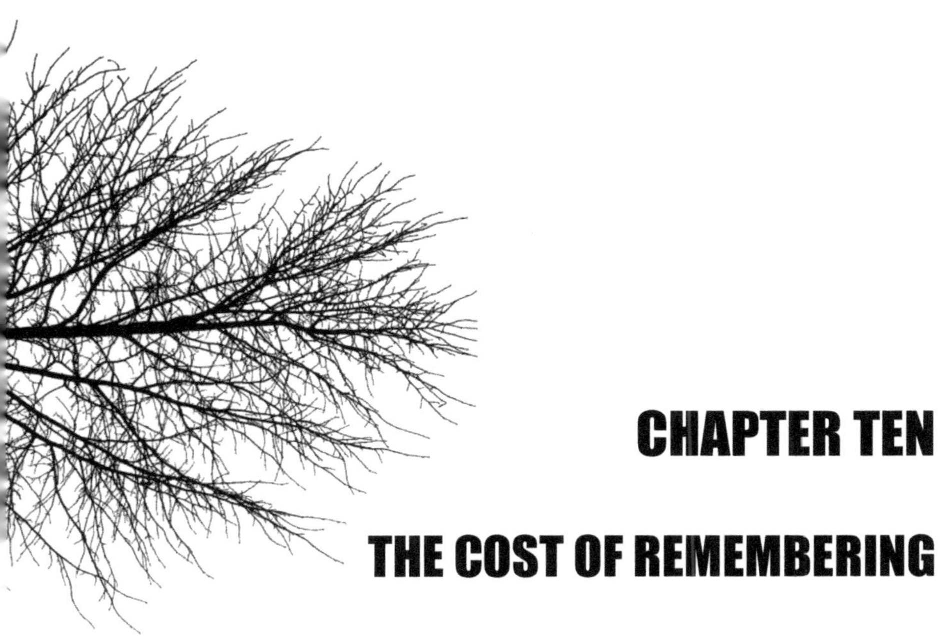

CHAPTER TEN

THE COST OF REMEMBERING

The journey back from the Ashen Wastes was a funeral procession of two. Arthur stumbled through the skeletal forest, Fig a fragile, fading weight in his arms. The little Echo-Folk's form, once a vibrant tapestry of moss and shadow, was now translucent at the edges, its light guttering like a candle in a draft. Arthur could feel the faint, feverish tremors that ran through its small body. The mental link between them was reduced to a faint, staticky hum, like a distant radio signal. Each flicker of Fig's form felt like a piece of the world itself dying.

He carried two precious, impossible things: the True Name of the First Star, a constellation of meaning burning with quiet intensity in his mind, and the living creature who had nearly sacrificed its own existence to save him. The Name was power, but it was cold comfort against the warmth of the friend he was losing.

The grey dust of the Wastes clung to his clothes and skin,

a gritty reminder of the void they had escaped. Each step away felt like a hollow, pyrrhic victory. He had stared into the face of the Alchemist and seen his own non-existence reflected back. The memory of that static hand was seared onto his retinas—a chill that had settled deep in his marrow, a permanent winter in his soul.

He walked for hours, his body a landscape of aches. Though the Glimmerwood around him slowly regained its color, the vibrancy seemed muted, the sorrowful hum of the memories tinged with a new, desperate note. He had walked through the end of things, and the path there was not fiery and dramatic, but quiet, grey, and utterly passive.

When the familiar, sheltered clearing finally came into view, Arthur nearly wept with profound relief. He pushed through the silver willow branches and collapsed to his knees at the base of the Heartwood. Gently, he laid Fig down in a sheltered nook where the moss was thickest and the tree's hum was strongest.

The Heartwood seemed to sense their distress. The opal leaves rustled in a silent, sympathetic breeze. The patch of bark healed by the musical note still glowed, a small bastion of health. But the tree recognized the victory had come at a cost.

"Fig," Arthur whispered, his voice cracking. "We're home. We're safe."

The Echo-Folk's eyes fluttered open, their light dim, the vibrant amber faded. It tried to raise a hand, but the effort was too much. A weak, fragmented thought reached Arthur, brittle as old parchment....costly... the memories... I poured too many of yours back into you... to shield you... my own song is thin...

Arthur understood with a sickening lurch. Fig had used Arthur's loud, chaotic human memories as a shield against the Alchemist. In doing so, it had drained its own essence, woven from the quiet, refined echoes of the Glimmerwood. It had traded its ancient, specialized currency for his human one, and was now bankrupt.

"What can I do?" Arthur asked, desperation clawing at him. He looked around the clearing at the Last Things. "How do I help you?"

Fig's gaze, weak but unwavering, drifted towards the collection. A specific feeling, thin and frayed, pointed toward the chipped teacup....an echo of warmth... not a memory... a feeling... I need to remember... warmth...

Arthur scrambled over and picked up the teacup. It was cold and inert. He closed his eyes, straining to feel the echo Fig needed, but his own resonance felt dull, blunted by terror and the immense, cold weight of the True Name in his mind. He was a radio tuned to a station of cosmic power, and he couldn't find the frequency for a simple, comforting warmth. He pushed, he strained, but the cup was silent.

Panic rose in his throat. He was failing. He had the power to restore the great Foundational Cores of the universe, but he couldn't find a simple feeling of warmth to save his friend. The irony was cruel and devastating.

He looked from the dying Fig to the Heartwood. He had the Second Core, a word that could call a star into being. But it was useless for this. It was a thing of definition, of cold, hard truth. It had no warmth.

This required not the power of a Warden, but the empathy

of a boy.

He did not try to pour the Name into the Heartwood. Instead, he knelt before Fig. He placed one hand on the Echo-Folk's cool, fading brow, and the other he pressed flat against the mossy earth, connecting them both to the land.

He closed his eyes. He let go of the fear, the exhaustion, the cosmic importance of the True Name. He focused on the simplest, purest, warmest memory he possessed.

It was not a memory from the Glimmerwood. It was from his own world. A memory so small and quiet he had almost forgotten it.

It was a Saturday morning, years ago. He had climbed into his parents' bed, slipping into the warm space between them. The morning sun was filtering through the curtains. It was warm. It was safe. There was only the steady, rhythmic sound of their breathing, and the profound, unshakeable certainty that he was loved. It was a memory of a state of being. A feeling of absolute, unconditional safety.

It was not a loud memory. It did not shimmer or pulse. It was a small, golden, perfect thing.

And he gave it away.

He did not hum. He did not sing. He simply offered it with an open heart, to the clearing and to his friend. He poured this feeling of pure, safe warmth into his resonance and let it flow out of him, a gentle, healing tide.

He felt a shift. A gentle sigh ran through the entire clearing. The moss under his hand glowed a deeper, more vibrant green. The air grew a fraction warmer. A faint, corresponding warmth emanated from the chipped teacup nearby, its own stored echo of companionship kindled.

More importantly, he felt a tiny, answering flicker from Fig. A spark of warmth, mirroring his own. The Echo-Folk's form solidified, just a little. Its large eyes found his, filled with a deep, profound kinship. He had not just given it energy; he had shared an experience. He had given it a piece of his own humanity.

You... Fig's thought was a soft, wondering breath, stronger now....you shared your own... you did not give me an echo... you gave me a piece of your sun...

Arthur, his eyes stinging with tears, simply nodded. He had learned a new lesson: Restoration was not just about reinforcing what was lost from the outside. It was about sharing what you had from the inside. It was about connection, not just correction.

For a long time, they sat in silence, drawing strength from the quiet and from each other. Arthur understood the true cost of this war. It wasn't measured in grand battles, but in the slow, steady erosion of self—in the pieces of your soul you had to give away to keep other souls from fading.

Finally, when Fig was strong enough to sit up, Arthur turned to face the Heartwood. "It's time," he said.

He approached the magnificent, ailing tree. He placed his hands upon a section of bark that was grey and cracked, a map of the Glimmerwood's identity crisis. He closed his eyes and reached into the vault of his mind, where the True Name of the First Star blazed like a captured sun.

He did not speak it aloud. He simply held it in his thoughts, focused on its perfect, runic pattern, its absolute definition, and offered it to the tree, as he had offered his memory to Fig.

The effect was not a wave of golden sound, but something deeper, more fundamental. A ripple of certainty moved through the clearing. The very light seemed to sharpen, the colors becoming more true, more themselves. The cracks in the bark beneath his hands sealed with a soft, grinding sound, like stone settling into its rightful place after an age of doubt. The opal leaves above shimmered, their light burning steadier, casting clearer, more defined shadows.

A feeling of profound identity washed over Arthur. For a moment, he knew, with absolute clarity, exactly who he was. He was Arthur Pensive, the Restorer. He was the boy who remembered. He was the Warden of the Balance.

As the feeling faded, leaving behind a deep, resonant peace, he looked at Fig. The creature was standing, its strength returning. But its gaze was troubled, looking out toward the Glimmerwood beyond.

A new thought formed in Arthur's mind, clear and cold as ice. They had won two great victories. They had baffled the Alchemist and restored two Cores. But they had also revealed the full extent of Arthur's power. They had shown the Alchemist that he was not just an anomaly, but a direct threat to its purpose. An active, creative, restorative force in its universe of subtraction.

The Alchemist, a force of pure, logical entropy, would now be recalculating. It would no longer see Arthur as a mere curiosity. It would see him as the primary obstacle to its purpose. The next time they met, there would be no hesitation.

CHAPTER ELEVEN

THE ARCHIVE OF FALLEN KINGDOMS

For three cycles of the Glimmerwood's eternal twilight, Arthur and Fig did not leave the sanctuary. The Heartwood's clearing was now a crucible where Arthur forged a new understanding of his power, learning that his resonance was not a single note, but a symphony within him. Fig, fundamentally changed and fortified, moved with a grim, focused stillness.

The Alchemist does not sleep, Fig began, its thought-voice heavy with the gravity of a falling stone. It learns. Your resonance is a language it is now deciphering. It has analyzed your silent infiltration at the Shore and felt your defiance. Our final move cannot be one of stealth or silence. It must be an active, internal confrontation.

A new map unfolded in Arthur's mind, vaster and more

desolate than the Shore. He saw crumbling spires of obsidian piercing a blood-red sky—the Archive of Fallen Kingdoms, the graveyard of ambition and power.

The third Core is there. It is the First Act of Kindness. The spark that started the chain of empathy. It is the most powerful Core, for it is the antithesis of the Alchemist's nature—it is connection, not separation.

Arthur watched as the mental image zoomed in on the heart of the archive, a great, circular mausoleum. Guarding its entrance was a swirling, chaotic storm of negative emotion— the aggregated echo of every betrayal, cruelty, and selfish thought. It was a Sentinel of Hatred, a mindless, raging barrier that fed on compassion and selflessness.

The Alchemist knows the First Act of Kindness is the key to its undoing, Fig explained. It cannot approach the Core itself. So it has cordoned it off with this anti-empathy, a wall of distilled malice. To reach the Core, you must pass through the Sentinel. You cannot fight hatred with force or argue with rage. You can only disarm it with understanding.

The plan was terrifying in its simplicity—a psychological ordeal. Arthur would have to walk directly into the storm of concentrated hatred. He would have to open his resonance, allow every bitter echo of betrayal and rage to flood into him, absorb its pain, and reflect back compassion. It was a psychic trial that could shatter a mind forever.

"The Alchemist will be waiting, won't it?" Arthur asked, his voice quiet. "It will know the moment I try to calm the Sentinel. It will feel the shift in the emotional frequency".

Yes, Fig's confirmation was grim, final. That is my role. While you face the storm within—the battle for your own soul—I will face the silence without. I will make myself the loudest, most complex, most infuriatingly memorable thing in this entire realm. I will be the flare that blinds it while you perform the surgery.

"No!" The protest was instinctive, visceral. "It will erase you. It sees us now. It won't be baffled again. It will focus everything on you and unmake you".

Fig looked at him with a gaze of sorrowful, absolute resolve. I am not the same as I was. You changed me. I carry echoes of your human strength, your stubborn will, your beautiful, messy, chaotic noise. I am Fig, your friend. And if my purpose is to be the shield that allows the sword to strike true, then I will be that shield. Gladly.

The resolve in those thoughts was unshakeable. Arthur saw the strategy now: a coordinated assault on two fronts. He was the scalpel, tasked with a delicate, precise, internal operation. Fig was the shield, who would draw the blade and ring like a bell, drawing all enemy fire.

They prepared with solemn intensity. Arthur sat alone, practicing building mental fortifications—not walls to block the hatred, but channels, allowing the negative emotions to flow through him without pooling or drowning. He had to understand the storm without becoming the storm.

Fig, meanwhile, absorbed complex fragments of stories from the Last Things: the enduring love from the locket, the adventurous spirit from the boat, the comforting warmth from the teacup. Its form grew more layered, a walking tapestry of everything worth saving. It was making itself into the most compelling story the Glimmerwood had ever told, one the Alchemist would be unable to ignore.

When the time came, they stood together at the edge of the clearing. The path to the Archive was a road of black, polished stone that swallowed the light—a road of endings.

"Ready?" Arthur asked.

For the Glimmerwood, Fig thought.

For the Quiet Things, Arthur replied in his own mind.

Together, they stepped onto the black road and began the long, dark journey, their fates more intertwined than ever before.

CHAPTER TWELVE

THE SENTINEL AND THE STORM

The road to the Archive of Fallen Kingdoms was a journey through a land in the final, gasping throes of being forgotten. The black, polished stone of the path felt unnervingly smooth and cold, as if worn down by eons of spectral feet marching towards oblivion. The melancholic beauty of the main Glimmerwood was a distant dream. The trees that lined their way were petrified into grotesque, twisted shapes, their branches frozen in eternal screams of silent agony. The air was thick, tasting of old metal, ash, and a profound, collective sorrow that clung to the back of Arthur's throat.

He saw the ghosts of the kingdoms themselves. Not as shimmering memories, but as vast, translucent after-images superimposed over the bleak landscape—a palimpsest of fallen glory. He walked through the crumbled foundation of a fortress wall, and in the next moment, saw the wall whole and towering, manned by soldiers whose faces were blurred smudges of determination. He heard the faint, chaotic symphony of a bustling city market—the clink of coins, the shouts of merchants, the laughter of children—all layered over a deathly silence. It was a place of profound cognitive dissonance, where the past refused to die a clean death, lingering as a tortured, unresolved echo.

Fig moved beside him, a small, focused point of solidity in the chaotic haze. Its form was pulled taut, its usual flickering subdued into a low, protective glow. Its communication was sparse and tactical, a series of sharp, clear images pointing out unstable psychic ground or pockets of corrosive sorrow. Fig's mind was a razor-sharp compass navigating this emotional minefield.

The Archive's heart is close, Fig's thought cut through the ghostly din of a thousand-year-old coronation ceremony. The Sentinel will feel our approach. It is not a thinking thing, but a feeling one—a wound that has become a weapon. Remember, Arthur. Do not build a wall. Build a sieve. Let the hatred pass through you, understand its origin, but do not let it make a home within you. Your core is kindness. That is your anchor.

Arthur nodded, jaw tight. He practiced, in small ways, as they walked. He let the edge of a ghostly noble's paranoid jealousy brush his mind. Instead of recoiling, he followed the feeling to its source: a deep, festering insecurity, a fear of being overlooked, a childhood of never being good enough. The jealousy didn't vanish, but its sharp edge dulled, becoming a sad, understandable flaw rather than a monstrous, external force. It was exhausting, delicate work, and this was only the background radiation of the place.

Soon, the ghostly cities gave way to a vast, open plain under a sky the color of a fresh bruise, a swirling maelstrom of purple, black, and sickly yellow. In the center stood the Archive itself—a colossal, spiraling structure woven from the solidified memories of the fallen kingdoms. Before it, guarding the great, dark entrance that looked like a mouth ready to swallow hope, was the Sentinel.

It was exactly as Fig had shown him, yet the reality was a thousand times more visceral. It was a swirling, furious maelstrom of dark, violent colours—indigos of betrayal, crimsons of rage, sickly greens of envy—all swirling in a chaotic dance of pain. It had no form, but its voice was a cacophony of silent screams and curses that pummelled Arthur's mind, a psychic hurricane seeking to scour away all light and hope. It was the emotional residue of every fallen kingdom, given a terrible, mindless life.

I will draw the Alchemist now, Fig's thought was calm, the eye of the hurricane. Do not falter, Arthur Pensive. The Glimmerwood's heart beats with yours. Remember the warmth. Remember the sun.

Before Arthur could respond, Fig stepped into the center of the plain. The little Echo-Folk stopped trying to be small. It drew itself up and began to shine. It pulled on the threads of power it had gathered, and its form erupted in a kaleidoscope of light and memory. It became a living prism, projecting a dizzying, rapid-fire barrage of the Glimmerwood's most vibrant, defiant echoes—a fireworks display of meaning. It was shouting, "HERE I AM!" to the silence.

The effect was instantaneous. The fabric of the air before Fig began to tear. A soundless rip in reality, a seam of static and non-light. From this tear, the Alchemist emerged. It was simply there, its presence an immediate and absolute subtraction from the world. The ghostly sounds of the plain around them ceased. The Alchemist's full, terrifying attention was now locked on the small, defiantly shining creature. The static of its form churned with aggressive intensity. This was a targeted deletion.

This was it. No more time for fear. Arthur turned his back on the confrontation and faced the storm. He took a deep, shuddering breath and walked directly toward the Sentinel.

The moment he crossed an invisible threshold, the world vanished. All was blotted out by the raging storm in his mind. It was like being plunged into a freezing, black ocean made of pure malice.

You are weak, a voice that was a million voices hissed in his skull, the collective memory of every betrayer. You trust, and you will be broken. Your kindness is a flaw. Look at your friend out there! He burns brightly now, but he will be extinguished! And you will be alone again!

Images, vivid and painful, assaulted him. He saw Fig dissolving into static under the Alchemist's relentless touch, its stories unwritten. He saw his parents turning away from him in active disgust. The pain was excruciating, a cold fire in his veins.

His instinct was to fight back, to build a wall. But he

remembered Fig's words: A sieve, not a wall. He remembered the citadel of his core self.

He let the images come. He let the voices scream. He did not fight them. Instead, he reached for his resonance—the memory of the warm bed, the feeling of the completed symphony—and began to understand the storm. The hatred was not a primary force; it was a reaction. It was the scar tissue over profound wounds. The betrayal stemmed from broken trust. The rage from utter powerlessness. The envy from a hollow feeling of lack. These were not monsters; they were children of pain.

He did not reflect the hatred back. He reflected understanding. I see your pain, he thought, not as a weapon, but as a balm, a key offered to a locked room. He projected the memory of his own loneliness, a personal echo of their vast, historical suffering. I have felt a shadow of this. It is a cold house to live in. It does not have to define you.

The storm recoiled. The chaotic screams faltered, the rhythm of the malice broken. The hatred had no defense against compassion, against being seen and understood. It was like throwing water on a grease fire; it sizzled and popped violently, then began to recede, its form losing coherence. The path to the Archive's entrance, once blocked by fury, was now clear, the Sentinel reduced to a confused, swirling mist, its violent colours softened to a sad, grey pallor.

Meanwhile, in the real world, Arthur saw only the clear, dark entrance to the Archive. He dared a glance back.

Fig was a blazing star against the Alchemist's oppressive

grey. But the Alchemist was learning, adapting. It was no longer trying to unmake Fig all at once. Instead, it was carefully, methodically, unpicking the threads of memory that composed it. A piece of Fig's light would flicker and vanish. Fig was being systematically taken apart—a slow, meticulous disassembly. And it was doing it without ever taking its attention from Arthur, still oriented toward the Archive, waiting for him to emerge.

They were running out of time. The shield was cracking.

CHAPTER THIRTEEN

THE FIRST KINDNESS

The silence within the Archive was a physical weight, heavier and more profound than any Arthur had ever known. It was the silence of finality, of stories shelved in a library where no one would ever read them again.

He had no time for awe or sorrow. The image of Fig's light being systematically erased by the Alchemist was a fire scorching the back of his mind, a desperate timer counting down in his soul. He ran, his footsteps echoing with a hollow, sacrilegious loudness in the profound stillness.

He stumbled into the vast, circular chamber—the heart of the Archive—and felt it. Not a powerful, blazing signal, but the exact opposite: a tiny, impossibly faint whisper of warmth. It was so small, so humble, so utterly out of place amidst the grand tragedy of the place. It was a feeling not of kings or empires, but of a single, simple gesture.

He followed it, his resonance latching onto that thread of warmth like a lifeline, turning away from the monuments to power and failure. He pushed through a low, hidden archway into a small, nondescript alcove.

Hovering just above a ghostly impression in the stone floor was the Third Core. It was a soft, golden, pulsing light, no larger than a dewdrop, yet containing a universe of meaning. He felt a single, profound sensation, a memory before memory: the moment one being, for the very first time, had seen the suffering of another and had chosen to alleviate it. The First Act of Kindness.

As he reached for it, a final, desperate defense from the Archive struck him—a psychic feedback loop of ultimate futility. He was flooded with the memories of all the times kindness had failed. A tidal wave of despair whispered, *Why bother? It is all for nothing in the end.*

Arthur staggered under the weight of it. This was the quiet, logical conclusion of a universe without meaning. He looked at the tiny, golden light, so fragile against the crushing, historical evidence of indifference.

He found his answer not in his mind, but in the memory of the warmth he had shared with Fig in the clearing. He did not argue with the memories. He accepted them. Then, he focused on the tiny, golden light.

"Because of this," he whispered, his voice clear in the dead silence of the alcove. He poured his conviction—that stubborn, illogical, beautiful hope—into his resonance, aiming it directly at the Core. "However many times it fails, the choice to try again is what matters. This is the first choice. And it matters."

His resonance, tuned to understanding, met the Core's pure frequency of empathy, and they harmonized. The wave of despair shattered against the unshakeable truth of that first, foundational act. The golden light brightened, pulsing with a gentle, unwavering strength. It settled softly into the palm of Arthur's hand. It felt not heavy or powerful, but like a promise.

He had it. The final Core.

He turned and ran, the Core cradled protectively in his hand, its gentle warmth seeping into his skin, a direct counterpoint to the cold dread in his heart.

He burst out of the Archive's entrance. The Sentinel of Hatred was a confused, swirling mist behind him, its storm of malice dissolved by his active compassion.

The scene that met his eyes was one of devastating, methodical loss. Fig was on its knees, its brilliant, kaleidoscopic light almost entirely gone. Its form was faint, barely more than a sketch, flickering in and out of existence.

The Alchemist stood over it, a hand of static extended, poised for the final, erasing touch. It had almost won. It had calculated the cost of unmaking Arthur was too high, so it had chosen to unmake his reason for being instead.

The Alchemist sensed Arthur immediately. Its featureless head turned. The static of its form churned with a new, chilling intensity. It saw the Core. It understood the threat.

Arthur didn't hesitate. He walked forward, directly

towards the Alchemist, the First Act of Kindness held before him like a shield. Its gentle light pushed back the edges of the oppressive grey.

This was not a shout. It was a statement of being.

Arthur did not attack. He simply presented the Core, the ultimate, undeniable evidence that connection mattered more than subtraction. He and Fig had endured its silence, defied its logic, and now they presented the one truth it could not erase: the pure, founding empathy of the world.

The confrontation had reached its final point.

CHAPTER FOURTEEN

THE RECONCILIATION

The moment stretched, thin and taut as a spider's silk over a bottomless chasm. Arthur's arm, extended with the pulsing Core, did not waver, though primal, human fear screamed in his skull. He was offering the very essence of connection to the embodiment of disconnection.

Fig stood beside him, now a being solidified from compassion itself. Its light was steady, a calm, watchful presence, a testament to the Core's power. Fig did not interfere, understanding this was a threshold Arthur alone must cross— a negotiation between fundamental forces that he, as the Resonant, the Bridge, had been chosen to mediate.

The Alchemist remained motionless, a statue of static and nullity. The chaotic churn of its form slowed to a faint, perplexed shimmer. For an entity whose sole function was the elegant, logical subtraction of existence, this offering—pure, irrational addition—was an impossible equation.

Then, something impossible happened.

A sound.

It was not from the Glimmerwood. It was a new sound, born in the space between Arthur's offering and the Alchemist's silence. It was the note Arthur had sung in the mists, now stripped of fear, refined into a statement of pure being. It was the sound of Arthur's resonance, reflected back not as an echo, but as an understanding.

The First Act of Kindness flared, its gentle golden light intensifying in recognition. It did not attack the Alchemist's silence; it began to weave through it. Threads of golden light, delicate as spider silk and strong as adamant, reached out and touched the Alchemist's static form.

Where they touched, the static did not vanish. It changed. The grey, formless void began to resolve into patterns. Faint, shimmering geometries emerged, like frost crystals forming on a windowpane. The crushing, passive indifference transformed into a different kind of quiet—not the silence of absence, but the silence of deep listening, the space between musical notes. The hollow, rhythmic knocking softened, becoming a slow, steady, resonant pulse, like the heartbeat of the world in its dormant, winter phase.

The Alchemist was not being destroyed. It was being re-contextualized.

A new understanding, vast and humbling, flooded Arthur's mind. The Alchemist was not the enemy. It was the necessary counterweight. It was the force that made memory precious by ensuring it was not infinite. It was the gentle hand that cleared away the clutter of forgotten moments to make space for new ones. The Great Amnesia was not malevolent; it was a cosmic recycler of spent light.

But it had grown unbalanced because the world of the Loud Ones had stopped creating meaningful new memories. Arthur, by restoring the Cores and offering understanding instead of defiance, had not defeated the Alchemist. He had reminded it of its true purpose.

The Alchemist, now a being of intricate, silent patterns and a soft, golden pulse, slowly bowed its head—a gesture of acknowledgment, of acceptance. It was a bow to the Balance. Then it took a step back, its presence diminishing, returning to its role as a necessary and balanced background process, its work no longer one of frantic consumption, but of mindful curation.

The effect on the Glimmerwood was a gentle, pervasive healing, a great sigh of relief. The grey, skeletal trees of the Ashen Wastes did not burst into vibrant life; their forms settled into dignified, silver monuments to what had been lost, their endings now honored. The Glimmerwood was at rest. It was a museum, not a hospice.

The Balance was restored.

Arthur let out a breath he felt he had been holding for a lifetime. The Core was gone, returned to the fabric of reality, its principle woven back into the heart of things.

He turned to Fig. The Echo-Folk, its eyes now the color

of deep, peaceful earth, was whole and steady.

You did not fight the silence, Fig's thought came, warm and clear. You sang a duet with it. You showed it its part in the song.

"We all did," Arthur said, his voice hoarse but steady. He knelt, and for a long moment, boy and Echo-Folk rested their foreheads together, a silent communion of two friends who had not just saved a world, but had helped it remember how to save itself.

The Threshold will remain, Fig communicated. The Key is yours. You are the Warden of the Balance now. This world and your own are linked through you. Your work is not over. It has just changed its nature.

Arthur Pensive turned, placed the Key against the bark of the great oak, and stepped through the Threshold, carrying the quiet peace of the mended magic within his soul, ready to face the noise of his own world, not as an escape, but as a mission.

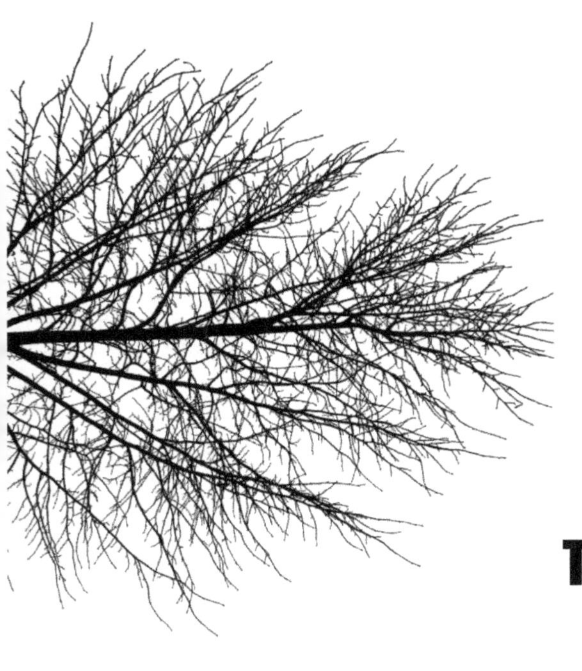

CHAPTER FIFTEEN

THE WARDEN OF THE BALANCE

The transition back was not a step, but a sigh. The profound, whispering peace of the restored Glimmerwood was replaced by the damp, earthy chill of an English night.

Arthur stood for a long moment, his hand still pressed against the rough, familiar bark of the oak tree. The Key in his palm was warm, a steady pulse against his skin, a tangible link to the reality he had just left. He pulled it away, and the doorway was gone. The tree was just a tree again, ancient and solid, holding its secrets deep within its rings. But he knew the cathedral that existed just behind the bark.

He looked down at himself. A small, glowing fragment of bioluminescent moss was caught in the cuff of his trousers, its soft green light a defiant spark in the ordinary darkness. He was a piece of that other world, standing here in this one. The disconnect was dizzying, but it was no longer frightening. It was his reality. He was the bridge.

He slipped in through the back door, the hinge giving its familiar, complaining squeak.

The house was quiet. He could hear the faint, rhythmic clicking of his mother's keyboard from her study upstairs, and the low murmur of a documentary coming from his father's den. It was the same as it had always been, a symphony of separate lives being lived in parallel.

But Arthur was listening with new ears, a Restorer's ears. He could hear the silence between the sounds—the hollow echo in the hallway that yearned for laughter, the quiet desperation in the relentless tapping of the keys. His own home was a landscape suffering from a subtle Amnesia of its own, a forgetting of how to connect.

He climbed the stairs to his attic room. His room was exactly as he had left it. He picked up the smooth, grey stone from his windowsill—the one that matched the one in his pocket. It was no longer just a stone. He could feel its story now, the millions of years it had lain in a riverbed, a tiny, solid testament to time. He was surrounded by quiet things, and he now understood that every single one of them was singing its story in a language only he was fluent in.

He was the Warden of the Balance. The title settled on him not as a burden, but as a fundamental truth, as intrinsic as the color of his eyes. It was not about grand, cosmic gestures. It was about this. It was about here. His first ward was not a forest of memories, but a quiet house on a quiet street.

The First Act of Warden-ship

The next morning, he went down to breakfast. His mother was scanning an academic journal, a half-eaten piece of toast forgotten. His father was frowning at his tablet, scrolling through financial news.

"Morning," Arthur said, his voice sounding strangely clear and solid.

His mother gave him a brief, absent smile before her gaze dropped back to the journal. His father grunted in acknowledgment.

The old loneliness threatened to descend like a familiar fog. But Arthur did not retreat. He remembered the First Act of Kindness. It was a choice, a simple turning towards another. It was a resonance.

He walked over to the counter and made a second cup of tea. He knew exactly how his mother took it. He set it down beside her elbow, gently moving the cold, forgotten cup aside.

"Your tea was getting cold," he said softly.

The action was so small, so mundane, yet it was a pebble dropped into the still pond of their routine. His mother looked up again, her focus truly landing on him for the first time.

"Oh," she said, her voice softer than he'd heard it in years. "Thank you, Arthur".

A tiny, resonant connection had been made. He had

reinforced a fading echo of care in his own home.

Later that day, he found his father in the garden, frustrated with a stubborn rose bush. "The secateurs are blunt," his father muttered.

Arthur walked to the garden shed, found the sharpening stone, and brought it out. He didn't offer to do the work. He just held the stone out. "Here".

His father took it, then nodded. "Sensible". They stood there for a minute, not speaking. The only sound was the rasp of metal on stone. It was not a conversation, but it was a shared moment. A collaboration. Arthur felt a flicker of the same harmony he'd felt when restoring the Cores. He was mending the broken threads of attention in his own home, using the quiet tools of presence and practical help.

This became his new practice. He did not try to explain the Glimmerwood. He simply lived the lessons he had learned. He listened, truly listened, when his parents spoke about their work, hearing not just the words but the buried passion or frustration within them. He began to notice the small, beautiful details they missed.

And slowly, almost imperceptibly, the house began to change. His mother started leaving her study door open. His father began asking his opinion on small things, genuinely listening to his answer. They were tiny shifts, but to Arthur, they were as significant as the healing of the Heartwood. He was using his resonance not on echoes, but on the living, present moment. He was the Warden of the Balance in his own home.

CHAPTER SIXTEEN

THE LEGACY OF NICHOLAS FROST

The picnic was a quiet revolution. It arrived not with banners and trumpets, but with the soft rustle of a tartan blanket, the clink of lemonade glasses, and the profound act of three people choosing to be together. The sun was a gentle, buttery gold, and the air hummed with the busyness of bees and the melodic chirping of sparrows. To Arthur, it was the most beautiful music he had ever heard, a symphony of the present moment, perfectly in tune.

His father, Dr. Alistair Pensive, had left his tablet inside. He sat on the blanket, his posture initially stiff, observing a ladybird navigate the vast terrain of a fold with the focus he usually reserved for structural schematics. "Remarkable navigators, ladybirds," he remarked. "Incredible efficiency of movement." It was a statement of fact, offered to the space between them as an invitation.

"She knows where she's going," Arthur said, leaning in to look. "Maybe she has a map we can't see."

His father glanced at him, a flicker of something close to a smile—a look of shared curiosity. "A cognitive map, perhaps. Imprinted at birth."

His mother, Dr. Eleanor Pensive, was lying back on the blanket, her face tilted to the sun. For the first time Arthur could remember, she was truly still. The tight, focused energy that usually crackled around her was quiet, replaced by visible relaxation. She sighed, a contented sound that seemed to release years of tension. "I'd forgotten how warm the sun feels," she murmured. "Out here, it's... it's a conversation."

Arthur felt a powerful swell of emotion. This was restoration. This was him using his resonance as a presence, creating a space where these small, healing moments could occur. His first, most important ward was the ecosystem of his own family.

As the afternoon wore on, the conversation meandered. His mother pointed out a cloud that looked like a sailing ship. His father told a halting story about trying to build a treehouse when he was ten. They laughed, a real, unforced sound that seemed to startle them all with its rarity and its rightness.

It was during a lull, as they packed the food away, that his mother looked at Arthur, her expression thoughtful. "This reminds me of your grandfather," she said, her voice soft. "Nicholas. He was the only one who could ever get me to just... sit. He'd tell me to 'listen to the garden'. I thought he was mad." She smiled, a distant, fond look. "But he'd point out the things you do. The way the light changes the colour of the leaves. He saw the world the same way you do, Arthur. Full of secret songs."

The name landed in Arthur's soul like a key clicking into a lock. Nicholas Frost. The previous owner of the Key. The warmth he'd felt from it wasn't just magic; it was a grandfather's love, waiting for the right hands to hold it.

"What was he like?" Arthur asked, his voice barely a whisper.

And so, sitting there on the grass, they told him. The stories were hesitant, rusty from disuse, but they began to flow. His mother spoke of a man with a laugh that could fill a room, a historian of places who believed every stone had a story. His father, to Arthur's astonishment, added details—how Nicholas had taught him how to whittle, how to identify constellations, how silence wasn't empty, but full.

"He called it 'the deeper listen,'" his father said, the words sounding strange and poetic in his practical mouth. "Said most people only heard the noise. But if you were quiet enough, you could hear the world humming its tune."

Arthur's heart was pounding. He was not an anomaly. He was a legacy. The Key had chosen him not by chance, but by blood, by a shared frequency of soul. The loneliness that had been his constant companion for so long suddenly had a context, a lineage. He was part of a tradition of listeners, of Wardens.

That night, settled into a new, softer quiet, Arthur climbed to the attic. He went straight to his grandfather's trunk. It was no longer a repository of forgotten things; it was an archive. He unbuckled the straps with reverence. He went straight for the large, leather-bound sketchbook at the bottom. He opened it.

The maps were even more incredible than he remembered. They were diagrams of wonder. He saw the "Ley Lines of Sunlight," the "Whispering Paths of the Wind." There was the "Dragon's Lair" under the hawthorn, the "Portal to the Star-Meadows"—the exact spot where the old oak tree stood.

But it was the notes in the margins that stole his breath. They weren't written in standard English, but in a flowing, elegant script that was part writing, part drawing. As Arthur focused, his resonance began to decipher them. They weren't words; they were feelings. A drawing of a spiralling shell was accompanied by the sensation of deep, ancient patience. A sketch of a dewdrop held the feeling of perfect, transient beauty. His grandfather hadn't just mapped the garden; he had mapped its soul. He had been a Resonant, just like Arthur.

And then, on the final page, he found it. A map of the Glimmerwood. It was titled "The Quiet Country." There was the quartz path, the stream of singing water, the Mists of Unheard Melodies labelled "The Vale of Lost Songs," the Ashen Wastes named "The Plains of Lethe." In the center, where the Twin Heartwoods stood, was a single, powerful sensation: Balance.

His grandfather had known. He had been there. He had been the Warden before him.

A final, separate note was tucked into the binding. As Arthur touched it, the meaning flowed directly into his mind, in a voice that felt both old and comfortingly familiar.

To the one who comes after,

If you are reading this, then the Key has chosen well, and the Balance endures. The Quiet Country is not a place you visit, but a part of you that you remember. Tend it, as you tend your own heart. Listen to its silences, as you listen to your own. The work is never done, for the noise of the world is loud and forgetful. But the quiet things remember. They always remember. Be their Warden. And know that you do not walk this path alone.

Nicholas

Arthur sat back, tears streaming down his face. They were not tears of sadness, but of homecoming. The last piece of his identity clicked into place. He was Arthur Pensive, grandson of Nicholas Frost, Warden of the Balance, heir to a magnificent legacy. The loneliness was gone, replaced by a connection that spanned generations and worlds.

He looked out the attic window. The Threshold was there. The Glimmerwood was there. His family was here. And he was the bridge between it all. He had a lifetime of sacred duty ahead. But for the first time, it didn't feel like a weight. It felt like a song, a beautiful, endless song that he was now a part of.

CHAPTER SEVENTEEN

THE WARDEN'S MAP

The discovery of his grandfather's legacy did not so much change Arthur's life as it explained it, providing historical and emotional context for the melody that had been playing in his soul since he was old enough to feel the quiet stories in stones. The loneliness that had once been a cold, hollow space inside him was now filled with a sense of lineage, a connection to a grandfather whose essence was woven into the very fabric of his being and the world he now helped protect. He was the latest in a line of listeners, a keeper of a sacred trust. This knowledge settled over him not as a burden, but as a well-fitting coat, warming him from the inside out.

This new understanding permeated every aspect of his life with a quiet, steady purpose. School was no longer a prison of noise, but a new kind of Glimmerwood, a complex landscape of human echoes he was learning to navigate with a Warden's discerning ear.

He understood Liam Carter now, not as a monster, but as a particularly loud, damaged echo. Liam's bravado was a fortress wall around deep-seated insecurity, a fear of being insignificant. Arthur's strategy shifted from avoidance to neutral presence. When Liam lobbed a snide comment his way in the crowded hallway, Arthur stopped. He met Liam's eyes with a calm, unflinching gaze that reflected not fear or anger, but a simple, unassailable fact: *I see you. And your words cannot change what I am.* The resonance was quiet, an internal note of unwavering self-possession. Liam stumbled, his sneer dissolving into genuine confusion. Deprived of the reactive fuel he craved, he quickly drifted away. Arthur had found the Dot of Liam's problem.

Arthur found his way back to the art room, to the quiet corner where Anya Sharma built worlds of graphite and imagination. He didn't try to make small talk, which felt like throwing pebbles into a deep, still well. Instead, he brought her an offering from his world: a smooth, black river stone, its surface veined with a single, lightning-bolt crack of white quartz.

He placed it beside her open sketchbook, where a magnificent, serpentine dragon was taking flight. "It looked like one of your dragon's scales," he said simply, his voice low so as not to disturb the creative silence of the room. Anya picked it up, her clever, charcoal-smudged fingers tracing the quartz vein. She looked from the stone to Arthur, her dark, intelligent eyes holding a thoughtful, appraising look. She did not speak, but Arthur felt a powerful current of shared recognition—a simple, instant understanding that required no explanation of Ley Lines or Glimmerwood. "It does belong to him," she murmured, her voice soft with immediate acceptance. A quiet bridge was built that day, not with words, but with a shared frequency of perception.

At home, the slow, gentle work of restoration continued. The picnic became a sacred, scheduled space where the only agenda was presence. His mother began cataloguing the family photographs, performing a historian's work of a deeply personal kind. His father began genuinely consulting Arthur on his garden plans.

"The horticultural texts all state that a rectangular bed is the most efficient use of space," his father said, tapping the screen with a stylus.

Arthur looked at the rigid lines on the screen, then out the window at the living garden. "But the sunlight moves in a curve," Arthur replied. "A rectangular bed fights the light. A curved one would... welcome it. It would be more... harmonious".

His father looked from the stark blueprint to the living garden beyond, a slow dawning in his eyes, a crack in his purely utilitarian worldview. "Harmonious," he repeated. He paused, tracing the curved line on the screen. "It's the fundamental elegance of simple facts," he added. "The efficiency of nature. You see the Dot of the problem, Arthur". It was a note of intuitive beauty chosen over cold utility. It was a restoration.

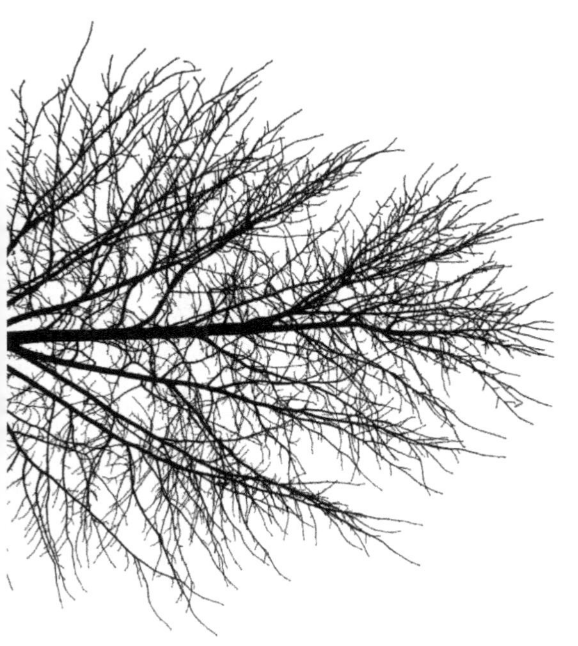

CHAPTER EIGHTEEN

THE FIRST ECHO

The new equilibrium was a living, breathing thing, as delicate and resilient as a spider's web after a morning dew. Arthur moved through his days with a dual awareness, his consciousness a gentle pendulum swinging between the mundane rhythm of school and home and the deep, resonant hum of the Glimmerwood. He was the fixed point, the fulcrum, and this quiet balancing act was becoming as natural to him as breathing. Yet, a true Warden knows that balance is not a static state to be achieved and forgotten; it is a dynamic dance, a constant series of minute adjustments in response to an ever-changing world. The first test of his stewardship arrived not with a roar, but with a whisper.

It began as a faint, dissonant itch at the edge of his perception, so subtle he initially mistook it for lingering fatigue. It persisted as he walked home—a sour note beneath the familiar symphony of his neighborhood's sounds. It was there at the dinner table, a grey static beneath the new, easier conversation with his parents. It felt like a memory of the Ashen Wastes, a ghost of the Amnesia, but it was here, in his world.

That night, in the sanctity of the Glimmerwood, he mentioned it to Fig. *The air in my world... it feels thin in one spot.* Near the old railway cut. There's a... a vacuum.

Fig paused, its form, now a stable tapestry of mossy greens and compassionate gold, stilled. *The Balance is a web,* it communicated, its thought-voice thoughtful. *A pull in one world creates a tension in the other.* A vacuum in your world does not simply sit in isolation. It draws. It hungers. *It will seek to be filled, and if not with good echoes, then with... other things.*

The old railway cut was a place Arthur knew well. It was a scar on the edge of town, a deep gash overgrown with weeds and littered with the ghosts of industry—rotting wooden ties, twisted scraps of metal, and the pervasive sadness of abandonment. It was a place the town had collectively decided to ignore. Arthur understood with cold clarity: that act of collective forgetting had created a pocket of potent Amnesia, a vacuum beginning to affect the very fabric of the Glimmerwood.

The following day, he went to the cut. Standing at its edge, the feeling was unmistakable. It was a spiritual cold spot on a warm day. The colours seemed washed out, the sounds muffled. It was a place that resisted story. He could feel it pulling at his mind, tempting him to forget why he had come, to just turn around. This was the Alchemist's legacy in his world—the spaces created by neglect and apathy.

He couldn't fight this with a song. He couldn't restore a Core here, for there was no foundational memory to reinforce. This was a different kind of restoration. This was creation. He had to fill the void himself.

He started small. The next afternoon, he returned with a trash bag. It was a quiet, personal act of Warden-ship. As he picked up the plastic bottles, rusty cans, and forgotten wrappers, he didn't just see refuse; he acknowledged the small, lost stories they represented—a discarded drink, a moment of carelessness—and then gently released them, cleaning the slate.

It was slow, tedious work. But as he worked, he began to hum, the same low, resonant hum he had used on the locket. He wasn't humming to an object, but to the place itself. He was humming the memory of the train that had once run here, the industry and purpose it represented. He was humming the potential for the place to be something new. He was filling the emptiness with intention.

A few days later, he brought a smooth, water-worn brick he'd found buried in the mud—a relic from the railway's past. He cleaned it and placed it carefully in a small clearing, a focal point. It was a small anchor.

He told Fig about it on his next visit. I'm trying to give it a new story. A small one. *But the emptiness is deep.*

Fig observed him, its luminous eyes soft. *You are not just a Restorer of what was, Arthur.* You are a Grower of what could be. This is the deeper magic. The Alchemist could only consume what already existed. You... you can create.

Fig led him to a part of the Glimmerwood he had never seen before, a sheltered grove thick with the scent of rich earth and possibility. *This is the Nursery,* Fig explained. *Here, the memories are not echoes of the past, but seeds of the future, tiny, glowing motes of potential waiting to take root.* You cannot take a seed from here. But you can learn its song. You can learn the song of beginning.

Arthur spent hours in the Nursery, just listening, letting the frequency of pure potential—the feeling of a blank page, a first step—wash over him. It was a nervous, excited, beautiful resonance. He learned its patterns, its rhythm.

He returned to the railway cut, not with a physical object, but with this new song in his heart. He stood in the center of the cleared space, the old brick a silent witness, and closed his eyes. He poured the resonance of the Nursery into the void. He simply poured the feeling of possibility into the emptiness. He hummed the song of beginning.

He felt a shift, subtle as a sigh. The oppressive, sucking feeling of the deficit lessened. The air didn't suddenly become warm and vibrant, but the bitter edge of its coldness was gone. It felt... neutral. Waiting. It was no longer resisting story; it was ready for one.

He knew the work was not done. It would take time, many visits, many small acts. But the crisis was averted. The void had been stabilized. He had not just protected the Glimmerwood from a pull of Amnesia; he had actively healed a wound in his own world.

He reported this to Fig. You see? The Balance is not a wall between worlds. It is a conversation. You have just spoken a new word into that conversation. A word of 'what if.'

That evening, as Arthur added a new page to his grandfather's sketchbook—a drawing of the railway cut, not as a scar, but as a gentle, open bowl, infused with the shimmering, light-green feeling of potential—he understood the full scope of his role. A Warden did not just stand guard. A Warden planted seeds. A Warden listened to the silences and, where they were barren, taught them how to sing.

CHAPTER NINETEEN

THE UNFINISHED SYMPHONY

The resolution of the railway cut was not an ending, but a profound deepening of Arthur's understanding. The vacuum had been neutralized, its hungry silence filled not with a shout, but with the patient, humming potential for a new story. He was not a soldier in a concluded war, but a gardener in a perpetual, ever-blooming spring. The Balance was a living system he tended, ensuring the symphony never fell into silence.

This new phase of his stewardship was characterized by a quiet, watchful rhythm. He noticed when a friendship was fraying, emitting a discordant, anxious frequency, and would sometimes leave a small, interesting stone on the desk of each person involved. He wasn't aiming to fix them; he was reinforcing the possibility of repair. His quiet friendship with Anya flourished in this soil of mutual understanding.

At home, the curved herb garden was planted, a graceful swirl that followed the sun's path so perfectly it seemed to have always been there. The fragrant scent on a warm afternoon was a calming, aromatic resonance. His father had begun building a small, elegant bird feeder, his blueprints replaced by the tactile reality of wood and glue. The relentless energy of the household had softened into a gentle, cyclical rhythm of tending and appreciating.

In the Glimmerwood, Fig showed him the ongoing, gentle evolution of the realm. In the Vale of Echoed Songs, the unresolved melodies had begun to harmonize with one another, creating entirely new, complex compositions. The Glimmerwood was growing, adapting, integrating the new echoes flowing from Arthur's world.

They walked back to the Twin Heartwoods, the braided trees pulsing with a steady, platinum light. *The Balance is strong,* Fig communicated. *It requires a Warden not to hold it still, but to listen for the faintest dissonance, to make the minute adjustments before they become great ruptures. The ongoing work of a Warden is the practice of preventative medicine, of daily wellness.*

On a crisp, clear Saturday morning, Arthur undertook a new project: asking his parents to see the railway cut. They stood at the edge of the neglected place.

Arthur simply nodded. "It is. But listen".

He opened his resonance, not in a focused beam, but as a gentle field around them. He shared the song of potential, the memory of the trains and the hope for what might yet be.

He felt his mother gasp softly beside him. "Oh," she whispered. "It's... it's not sad. It's... waiting".

His father was silent for a long time, sweeping his gaze over the cut. "It has good bones," he said finally. "With some terracing on that bank... and some native wildflowers... it could be quite... harmonious".

In that moment, Arthur had shared his resonance with them, and they had felt its truth. It was the most powerful restoration he had ever performed. They began planning the next sentence in the story of this place together.

That night, Arthur opened his grandfather's sketchbook. He drew the railway cut not as it was, but as a concept. He drew the terracing as strong lines of stability and the wildflowers as notes of life and future beauty. Overlaying it all, he drew the shimmering, green-gold feeling of potential, now intertwined with the distinct, separate but harmonious resonances of his mother's curious intellect and his father's practical creativity. It was a map of a family beginning a new story together. The symphony of his life was not unfinished because it was incomplete. It was unfinished because it was alive.

CHAPTER TWENTY

THE SEED OF DISCORD

The planning for the railway cut became a new, shared language for the Pensive family. Blueprints and botanical guides now shared the kitchen table with historical journals and lesson plans. Arthur's father, Alistair, calculated the precise angle for the terracing to prevent erosion, his engineer's mind finding a strange, beautiful poetry in the mathematics of stability. His mother, Eleanor, delved into local archives, unearthing the history of the railway line—the industries it served, the towns it connected, the lives it carried. She wasn't simply planning a garden; she was researching a resurrection. Arthur watched this unfold with deep, quiet wonder. This was the Balance in action, more profound than he had ever imagined. It wasn't just about preventing voids; it was about channeling the unique energies of his world into acts of creation. His father's logic and his mother's scholarship were becoming tools of restoration, their own forms of resonance.

A week after their first visit, the three of them returned to the cut with work gloves, trowels, and native wildflower seeds—Lupine, Columbine, and Yarrow, chosen by his mother for their hardiness and their long-forgotten meanings of imagination, fortitude, and healing. The autumn sun was warm on their backs as they began the simple, physical work of clearing a small patch for the first terrace.

It was as Arthur was turning the soil, his hands sinking into the cool, dark earth, that he felt it. It was a vibration, but not the welcoming hum of potential he had cultivated. This was a sharp, dissonant twang, like a piano string snapping. It felt like a cold spike of pain driven straight into the Heartwood. It wasn't coming from the cut itself, but from the direction of the Glimmerwood. It was a spike of panic, followed by a wave of confusion that was distinctly and unmistakably Fig's.

He dropped his trowel, his head snapping up.

"Arthur? What is it?" his mother asked, noticing his sudden tension.

"I... I just remembered," he stammered, his mind already halfway through the Threshold. "I promised... I have to go check on something. For a... school project. In the woods."

The old lie felt flimsy on his tongue, but his parents, their faces smudged with earth, just nodded. "Don't be long," his father said. "We'll save the seeding for you."

Arthur ran, driven not by fear, but by a Warden's urgency. The dissonant echo was already fading, but its aftertaste lingered—a psychic shriek that had no place in the

Glimmerwood's restored peace. He barely registered the journey, the fumbling for the Key, the step through the shimmering air.

He emerged into a Glimmerwood that looked, on the surface, as serene as ever. The opal leaves shimmered, the stream sang its gentle song. But the air was wrong. It was thick, charged with a frantic, buzzing energy. The usual contented whisper of the forest had been replaced by a low, anxious murmur.

Fig was waiting for him at the edge of the clearing, pacing, its form flickering with uncharacteristic agitation. Arthur! You felt it?

"What was that?" Arthur asked, his heart still thumping. "It felt like... an alarm."

It was a rupture, Fig communicated, its thoughts sharp with distress. But not from the outside. From within. In the Nursery.

The Nursery. The grove of potential, the place of beginnings. A cold knot tightened in Arthur's stomach. They ran.

The moment they entered the sheltered grove, the wrongness was palpable. The air, usually thrumming with the excited, light-green frequency of possibility, was now a chaotic swirl of conflicting colours. The tiny, glowing motes of future memories—the seeds—were no longer drifting peacefully. They were swarming, clumping together in aggressive, competitive clusters, their gentle light a harsh, glaring fight for dominance.

In the center of the grove, one seed had grown disproportionately. It was no longer a mote, but a pulsing, sickly-yellow orb the size of his fist, and it was loud. It emitted a relentless, psychic broadcast of a single, simplistic memory: the triumphant, crushing final note of a forgotten war anthem. It was a memory of absolute victory, of total domination, and it was trying to drown out every other potential, demanding to be the only story the Glimmerwood would ever tell again.

What is it? Arthur thought, shielding his mind from the aggressive broadcast.

It is a Memory-Seed of pure Ego, Fig's thought was grim. A memory that was not content to be a part of the tapestry. It desired to be the entire weave. It fed on the energy of the Nursery, on the potential of all the other seeds, and... it has begun to germinate.

"How? The Balance is restored! The Alchemist is... balanced!"

The Balance is not a cage, Arthur. It is an ecosystem. When you healed the great wounds, you created a surge of life, of energy. This... this is a weed. A particularly virulent one. It is not evil. It is merely... voracious. It is a part of nature, too. A part we did not anticipate.

This was a new kind of threat. Not a void of silence, but a cacophony of a single, arrogant story. Not an erasure, but a tyranny. He couldn't offer it understanding; it understood only dominance. He couldn't restore a balance that had never included it.

He looked at the pulsing, yellow orb, at the way it was bullying the softer, gentler potentials around it, and he knew what he had to do. This was not a task for a Restorer. This was a task for a Gardener.

The Warden's work, it seemed, was never done. It had only changed its shape.

CHAPTER TWENTY-ONE

THE PRUNING

The aggressive, warlike thrum of the Memory-Seed was a physical pressure in the Nursery, a dissonant chord that made the very air feel gritty and hostile. Arthur stood at the grove's edge, Fig a tense, flickering presence at his side. This was a violation of the peace he had fought so hard to win. The Alchemist's silence had been a chilling emptiness, but this was a profound perversion—a cancerous growth of noise, a solitary story attempting to shout down the chorus.

It cannot be reasoned with, Fig communicated, its thought-voice strained as it resisted the seed's dominating broadcast. It knows only one song: its own. And it demands that all else be its audience, forever silent.

"So, we... destroy it?" Arthur asked, the concept feeling foreign and violent in this place of creation. To unmake a memory, even a hostile one, felt too much like the Alchemist's work.

To destroy it would be to create another kind of vacuum, Fig replied, its luminous eyes fixed on the pulsing yellow orb. And violence would only reinforce its narrative of conflict. No. It must be... pruned. Contained. Its energy must be redirected, its story re-contextualized back into the whole, not allowed to consume the tapestry.

It was a gardener's task. Not to eradicate the weed, but to remove its ability to choke the other plants. The solution required not force, but precision. Not a shout, but a scalpel.

"How?" Arthur whispered, feeling the weight of this new responsibility. The Cores had been about pouring energy in. This was about carefully managing energy out.

Its strength is its simplicity, Fig explained, its form shifting as it analyzed the problem. It is a solitary, powerful note. You cannot fight one note with another; that only creates more noise. You must remind the other seeds of their own strength. You must conduct the Nursery.

Arthur closed his eyes, pushing past the aggressive thrum of the war anthem. He reached for his resonance, but this time, he did not project it outward. He turned it inward, into the grove itself, seeking out the other Memory-Seeds—the gentle, frightened motes of potential that were being bullied into silence.

He found them, their lights dimmed, their frequencies muted by the yellow orb's dominance. There was a seed that held the soft, pink potential of a first friendship. Another held the steady, blue hum of a skill patiently mastered. Another held the silver, sparkling feeling of a moment of pure, unexpected wonder. They were all there, cowed and suppressed.

He began, not with a song, but with a whisper. He amplified the faint, pink frequency of the friendship seed, weaving a thread of its gentle connection through the air, a counter-melody to the blaring anthem. It was fragile, almost immediately swallowed by the yellow noise. But he persisted. He turned to the blue hum of patience, reinforcing it, giving it a steady, rhythmic pulse. Then the silver sparkle of wonder, letting it chime like a tiny, defiant bell.

It was exhausting, meticulous work. He was not one instrument, but a whole orchestra's worth of conductors, trying to cue dozens of timid players to stand up to a roaring soloist. Sweat beaded on his forehead. The war anthem seemed to push back, growing louder, more arrogant.

It is working! Fig's thought was a spark of encouragement. You are reminding them they are not alone!

Fig joined him then, not by conducting, but by becoming a living shield. The creature moved between the aggressive seed and the smaller ones, its own complex, layered form—a tapestry of loyalty, adventure, and compassion—acting as a buffer. The yellow orb's broadcast crashed against Fig's multifaceted story and fragmented, confused by the complexity it encountered. It was a weapon designed to attack simple, isolated targets; against a woven community, it lost its focus.

Emboldened, Arthur pushed further. He began to weave their frequencies together. He helped the pink thread of friendship intertwine with the blue pulse of patience, creating a stronger, more resilient strand. He wove the silver chime of wonder into that, creating a chord that was joyful, steadfast, and magical. One by one, the other seeds of the Nursery, feeling this support, began to brighten, to hum more confidently.

A new sound began to emerge in the grove, not a single melody, but a complex, interweaving harmony of dozens of different potentials of love, discovery, sorrow, triumph, quiet contentment.

The yellow orb's single, dominating note was now just one voice among many. And a single voice, no matter how loud, cannot sustain a tyranny against a true chorus. Its broadcast didn't stop, but it changed. The triumphant war anthem began to sound... lonely. Then plaintive. Then, finally, it faltered, its aggressive thrum softening into a confused, and then a weary, hum. It was still a memory of victory, but it was no longer a weapon. It was just a story, once again, one thread in the vast and beautiful tapestry.

The pressure in the grove vanished. The air cleared, once again filled with the gentle, excited thrum of pure, cooperative potential. The Memory-Seeds drifted peacefully, the crisis averted. The yellow orb, now contained, pulsed with a softer, gold light, its energy re-integrated.

Arthur slumped to his knees, utterly spent. This had been a different kind of battle—a battle of fostering community against the force of ego. It had required a deeper, more nuanced understanding of his power.

Fig stood over him, its form steady and warm. You see? A Warden does not only fight monsters and fill voids. A Warden tends the garden. Sometimes, that means pulling a weed.

Sometimes, it means strengthening the flowers so the weed cannot thrive.

Arthur nodded, his breath slowly returning to normal. He looked around the peaceful Nursery. The Balance was not a passive state. It was active, dynamic, and required constant, gentle vigilance. It required a love for the entire chorus, not just the loudest soloist.

He had saved the Glimmerwood from silence. Now, he had saved it from a tyrant. The title of Warden grew ever more profound, and he knew, with a certainty that settled deep in his bones, that his education was far from over.

CHAPTER TWENTY-TWO

THE RIPPLE AND THE STONE

The silence in the Nursery, once the frantic harmony had settled, was profound. It was not the dead silence of the Ashen Wastes, but the deep, resonant quiet of a system restored to health, like the calm in a forest after a passing storm. Arthur knelt on the soft, mossy ground, his body trembling with a fatigue that was more spiritual than physical. Conducting the chorus of the Nursery had been like trying to hold a galaxy of thoughts in his mind at once, each one requiring a precise and gentle touch. Fig stood beside him, a steady, warm presence, its own light pulsing in a slow, relieved rhythm.

You have learned a new language, Fig communicated, its thought-voice soft with pride and exhaustion. The language of the gardener. It is a more subtle tongue than that of the restorer or the warrior.

Arthur could only nod, his throat tight with emotion. He looked at the Memory-Seeds, now drifting in their peaceful, interweaving dance. The once-threatening yellow orb was now just another participant, its golden light contributing to, rather than dominating, the symphony. He had not destroyed it; he had socialized it. The concept felt immensely powerful.

The return to his own world was a jarring transition. The crisp, magical air of the Glimmerwood was replaced by the damp chill of an English afternoon. He stumbled out from behind the oak tree, his clothes still smelling faintly of peat and ozone. The Key in his pocket felt warm, almost hot, as if humming with the residual energy of the confrontation.

He found his parents exactly where he had left them, kneeling by the first terrace of the railway cut. They looked up as he approached, their faces showing quiet concern.

"There you are," his mother said, brushing a strand of hair from her forehead with a muddy glove. "Your project must have been absorbing. You were gone quite a while."

"Is everything alright?" his father added, his gaze sharp and assessing. "You look... pale."

Arthur felt a pang of guilt. "It was... complicated," he said, which was the most honest thing he could manage. He picked up his trowel, the solid, earthy weight of it a comfort. "But it's better now."

He knelt beside them and began to work, the simple, repetitive motion of digging and turning the soil a grounding balm. As he worked, he quietly hummed the complex harmony he had conducted in the Nursery—not the aggressive yellow note, but the woven tapestry of blue patience, pink friendship, and silver wonder. He was using the memory of his success in one world to fortify his labor in another, pouring the frequency of communal life into the earth.

The effect was subtle, but palpable. The small patch of earth they were preparing became more receptive. The clumps of clay broke apart more easily. The scent of the soil seemed richer, more alive. His father, who had been meticulously measuring the terrace angle, paused and looked at the turned earth, a faint, uncharacteristic smile on his face.

"Good soil," he remarked, squeezing a clump in his hand and watching it crumble. "It has a good structure."

His mother, scattering the first of the Lupine seeds into a shallow trench, looked up at the sky. "It feels like it wants to grow here," she said, her voice soft with wonder. "It feels... hopeful."

Arthur felt a surge of emotion so strong it threatened to overwhelm him. They were feeling it. They couldn't hear the symphony, but they were responding to its frequency. His work in the Glimmerwood was directly enhancing his work here. The Balance was not a wall; it was a conduit.

They finished planting the first terrace as the sun dipped below the horizon, painting the sky in streaks of orange and purple. They packed their tools in a comfortable, shared silence, the kind that needed no words. The railway cut was no longer a forgotten scar. It was a work in progress, a sentence they were writing together in the story of their town.

That night, as Arthur lay in bed, the events of the day replayed in his mind. The aggressive Memory-Seed, the delicate act of conducting the Nursery, the quiet satisfaction of planting seeds with his parents. They were not separate stories; they were different verses of the same song. A Warden's duty was holistic. Strengthening the Glimmerwood strengthened his own world, and healing wounds in his own world, like the railway cut, prevented the formation of voids that could poison the Glimmerwood.

His thoughts were interrupted by a faint, new sensation. It was a gentle pull, not from the Glimmerwood, but from within his own house. A faint, sad, grey echo. It was coming from his father's den.

He slipped out of bed and padded downstairs, avoiding the creaking stair. The door to the den was ajar. In the dim light from the hallway, he saw his father sitting in his old leather armchair, not working, not reading. He was simply holding something small and metallic, turning it over and over in his hands. The air around him vibrated with a profound, quiet sorrow.

It was the silver pocket watch. His grandfather's watch. The hands, Arthur knew, were frozen at 11:11.

Arthur stood in the doorway, unseen. He didn't need to use his resonance to understand the emotion. It was a void, not of forgetting, but of a memory so sharp and painful it had become a silent, locked room in his father's heart. The memory of a loss he never spoke of. The memory of his own father.

This was not a void created by the Amnesia. This was a

human void, created by grief. And Arthur realized with a jolt that his work as Warden was not just about grand, cosmic balances or even community gardens. It was about this, too. The quiet, personal desolations that existed in every heart, in every home.

He didn't know how to heal this. He couldn't conduct a chorus for a single, locked-away pain. He couldn't plant a seed in this kind of emotional concrete. This was a different kind of silence altogether.

He retreated back to his room, the image of his father alone with the watch burned into his mind. The Key felt heavy in his pocket. He had faced down the Alchemist and tamed a tyrannical Memory-Seed, but the sight of his father's silent grief felt like a more formidable challenge. The Glimmerwood had shown him how to fill voids and prune aggressive growths. But what was the remedy for a sorrow so deep it had become a part of someone's foundation? How did a Warden tend to a heart?

He fell into a troubled sleep, the peaceful symphony of the Glimmerwood feeling very far away. The path of the Warden, he was learning, was infinite, and its next turn was leading him into the most complex and uncharted territory of all: the human heart.

CHAPTER TWENTY-THREE

THE WATCH AND THE WOUND

The memory of his father's solitary vigil haunted Arthur through the night, a quiet, grey specter at the edge of his newfound peace. He had faced cosmic emptiness and psychic tyranny, but the profound, human silence of grief felt like a different order of problem. It wasn't a void to be filled with noise, nor a weed to be pruned. It was a deep, petrified forest within a person, a landscape where time had stopped at the moment of loss. The frozen hands of the pocket watch were not just a mechanical failure; they were a testament to a heart that had, in some essential way, also ceased functioning at that same point.

The next morning, a subdued Saturday, the atmosphere in the house was different. The shared purpose of the railway cut project had created new warmth, but Arthur could now feel the old, cold foundations beneath it. His father was back at his tablet, but his focus was brittle, the usual deep concentration replaced by a shallow, distracted energy. The echo of the watch's sorrow lingered around him like a fine mist.

Arthur found himself at a loss. His resonance, his ability to listen and harmonize, felt useless here. How did you harmonize with a note that refused to sound? How did you offer empathy to a pain that had walled itself off from the world?

Seeking guidance, or perhaps just solace, he retreated to the Glimmerwood. He found Fig in the Weeping Grove, a part of the forest where memories were not joyful or sorrowful in a passing way, but were profound, crystalline structures of pure, enduring emotion—a deep blue spire of lifelong devotion, a shimmering, obsidian monolith of a betrayal never forgiven.

You are troubled, Fig communicated as Arthur approached. The peace we won in the Nursery is unsettled within you.

"It's my father," Arthur said, the words feeling too simple. He described the scene from the night before—the watch, the quiet, the palpable weight of a story that had never been allowed to end. "It's like a Memory-Seed, but one that's turned to stone. I don't know how to... to garden that."

Fig was silent for a long time, its attention drifting to the obsidian monolith nearby. A feeling of immense, ancient bitterness washed over them.

Some histories are not seeds, Fig finally replied, its thought-voice heavy with the wisdom of epochs. They are monuments. They are not meant to grow or change. They are meant to stand. To be witnessed. The pain is not in the object itself, but in the isolation around it. The story has become a fortress with no windows and a single, locked door. You cannot change the stone, Arthur. But you can sit outside the walls. You can show that it does not have to stand alone in the silence.

The meaning unfolded in Arthur's mind. This wasn't about healing or fixing. It was about companionship. It was about presence. His role wasn't to pick the lock on his father's grief, but to simply be there, to acknowledge the fortress without trying to storm it.

He returned home, the philosophical concept clear, but the practical application felt terrifying. How did you "witness" a monument during a casual conversation?

An opportunity presented itself that afternoon. His father was in his den, the door once again ajar. Arthur hesitated at the threshold, his heart pounding. He saw his father at his desk, the silver watch lying beside a set of blueprints. His gaze kept drifting back to it, as if pulled by a gravitational force.

Summoning all his courage, Arthur knocked softly on the doorframe. "Dad?"

His father looked up, startled. "Arthur. Come in."

Arthur entered, the space feeling charged and fragile. He looked at the watch, falling back on the only truth he had. "It's a beautiful thing," he said, his voice quiet. "Even stopped."

His father's eyes flickered with surprise, then something softer, more vulnerable. He picked up the watch. "It was his favorite possession," he said, the words seeming to cost him something. "He said it was... dependable. Even when it broke, it was dependable in its brokenness." A faint, sad smile touched his lips. "He had a strange way with words, your grandfather."

This was it. The first window in the fortress. Arthur didn't push. He simply nodded, pouring all his attention, all his resonant listening, into that simple gesture. *I am here. I am listening.*

His father looked from the watch to Arthur, and the professional, pragmatic facade completely fell away. What was left was just a man, a son, holding the ghost of his own father.

"He would take this watch out on his walks," his father continued, his gaze turning inward. "He'd check it, even though he knew it was wrong. He said it wasn't about the time. It was about the... the ritual. The reminder." He took a slow breath. "He died on a Tuesday. Right out there, in the garden. Just... sat down on the old bench and didn't get up."

The air in the room seemed to still. Arthur felt the weight of the moment, not as an oppressive force, but as a sacred thing. He was being entrusted with a piece of the monument.

"I found him," his father whispered, the words barely audible. "I was the one who found him."

And there it was. The core of the petrified forest. Not just the loss, but the trauma of discovery. The quiet that had grown around it was a silence of shock, of a story too big for a young man to process, so he had built a fortress of quiet practicality around it and never let anyone in.

Arthur didn't offer platitudes or apologies. He knew, with a certainty that came from the deepest part of his resonance, that words were too small for this. Instead, he took a step closer and simply stood beside his father, looking down at the watch in his hand. He shared the space. He witnessed the monument.

They stood like that for a long time, the silence no longer empty. It was full. It was filled with the unspoken story, with the shared presence of two generations of sons, with the ghost of a third.

Finally, his father took a deep, shuddering breath, as if surfacing from deep water. He placed the watch back on the desk, his movements slow, deliberate. He looked at Arthur, and his eyes, while still sad, were clearer than Arthur had ever seen them.

"Thank you, Arthur," he said, the words heavy with meaning that went far beyond the moment.

Arthur just nodded again. He had done his work as Warden. He had not restored anything. He had not fixed anything. But he had, perhaps, begun to gently clear the isolation from around the monument, allowing a little light to touch the ancient stone.

He left the den, his own heart feeling both heavy and incredibly light. The path of the Warden was indeed infinite, winding not only through magical forests, but through the quiet, wounded rooms of the human heart. And the most powerful magic, he was beginning to understand, was sometimes no magic at all. It was just the courage to stand, to listen, and to be present in the face of another's silence.

CHAPTER TWENTY-FOUR

THE UNFOLDING SEASON

The shared silence in the den was a seed in itself. It did not instantly transform the house into a place of laughter and light, but it altered its fundamental chemistry. The air felt less brittle, the spaces between words less charged with unspoken history. In the days that followed, Arthur watched his father with a Warden's quiet attention. The change was subtle, a series of minute adjustments in the emotional landscape, clear to Arthur's attuned senses as the shift from winter to spring.

The pocket watch did not vanish, but it migrated. It moved from the locked drawer or the solitary contemplation to the mantelpiece in the living room, where it sat beside a small, framed photograph of Nicholas Frost. The watch was no longer a secret relic of pain; it was a memorial, integrated into the family's shared space. Its presence was no longer a silent scream of loss, but a quiet acknowledgment of a life that had been.

His father began to speak of Nicholas in fragments, pieces of the monument offered not in a torrent of grief, but as small, deliberate gifts. Over dinner, he might mention, "Your grandfather never could grow decent tomatoes. Claimed they were too prideful." Or, while looking at the oak tree, "He carved his initials on the far side of that trunk when he was a boy. NF. Took me weeks to find them." Each snippet was a thread, slowly weaving the ghost of Nicholas back into the daily tapestry of their lives, not as a sorrow, but as a continuing presence.

This unfolding within the house had a direct and powerful effect on the world outside their walls. Their weekend work at the railway cut took on a new, deeper resonance. It was no longer just a project of ecological restoration; it had become, unconsciously for his parents, consciously for Arthur, an act of familial continuity. They were building Nicholas's bench anew in a different form.

One Saturday, as they were setting stones for the second terrace, his father paused, a flat, grey stone in his hand. He looked at it, then at Arthur.

"He would have liked this," his father said, his voice matter-of-fact, but the emotion underneath was as rich and dark as the soil they were turning. "The patience of it. The... the listening to the land."

Arthur felt a surge of warmth that had nothing to do with the autumn sun. This was the harmony he had conducted in the Nursery—the blue of patience, the pink of connection—now manifesting in his own world. He was witnessing the reintegration of a lost story.

"He's probably why I see it," Arthur said softly, taking a risk. He didn't look at his father, focusing instead on fitting a stone into the terrace wall. "The deep stuff. In things."

There was a long silence, filled only by the sound of a distant bird and the rustle of leaves. Arthur could feel his father's gaze on him.

"Yes," his father said finally, the single word carrying a universe of acceptance. "I suppose he is."

It was the closest they had ever come to acknowledging the shared legacy, the secret frequency that ran in their blood. No more needed to be said. The understanding was now a living thing between them, as real and present as the oak tree at the bottom of their garden.

That evening, Arthur brought this new, consolidated energy back to the Glimmerwood. He found Fig near the stream, but the creature was not alone. A smaller, fainter Echo-Folk, one Arthur had never seen before, was with it. This new one was a shifting, silvery thing, like a pool of quicksilver given tentative form, and it seemed to be learning from Fig, mirroring its movements.

This is Gleam, Fig introduced, its thought-voice touched with mentorship. It is newly formed from the strengthened echoes of your world. The Balance is not just stable, Arthur. It is generative. It is creating new life.

Arthur watched, awestruck, as Gleam attempted to reinforce a nearby memory-shimmer, its efforts clumsy but earnest. The Glimmerwood was not just healing; it was evolving, diversifying. His work, and the healing in his own home, was directly contributing to this renaissance.

He told Fig of the developments with his father, of the watch on the mantelpiece, of the shared silences that were now full instead of empty. You see? Fig's communication was a soft, proud hum. You tended the soil around the monument. You did not assault the stone. And now, life is growing at its feet. This is the way. This is always the way.

They walked together to the Twin Heartwoods. The grove was more magnificent than ever. The braided trees pulsed with a light that seemed deeper, more complex, as if they had absorbed the lessons of the recent trials. Remembering and Forgetting were not just in balance; they were in a dynamic, creative dance. Arthur could feel it—the Remembering was now laced with the gentle release of things that no longer needed to be carried so heavily, and the Forgetting was infused with the wisdom of what was truly essential to hold onto.

He placed his hands on the intertwined trunks. A double frequency flowed into him, warmer and more welcoming than ever before. It was no longer just a power to be wielded, but a partnership to be honored. He was not just the Warden of the Balance; he was a part of the Balance itself.

When he returned home, the house was quiet. His mother was reading on the sofa, the completed photo album beside her. His father was in his armchair, not working, but simply looking at the watch on the mantel, his expression thoughtful but no longer haunted.

Arthur did not go to the attic. He went to the living room and sat on the floor near his father's chair, pulling out his own sketchbook. He didn't draw the Glimmerwood or the railway cut. He began to draw the living room itself. He drew the lines of the mantelpiece, the shape of the watch, the intent look on his mother's face as she read. He poured into the drawing the feeling of this new, fragile, and beautiful peace—the quiet hum of a family that had, against all odds, found its way back to each other. He was charting a new kind of territory. The territory of home.

The autumn turned crisper, the days shorter. The first terrace of the railway cut was now a gentle arc of dark, rich earth, waiting under the winter sky. The project would pause until spring, but the intention was set, the story was begun. The Pensive household, too, entered a quieter season. But the quiet was different now. It was the quiet of contentedness, of understanding, of a shared journey being undertaken one gentle, resonant step at a time.

Arthur Pensive, the Warden, sat in the heart of his home, his two worlds—the magical and the mundane—finally, perfectly, in tune. The symphony was playing, and he was, at last, a part of the music.

CHAPTER TWENTY-FIVE

THE FIRST FROST

The peace that had settled over both of Arthur's worlds was not the fragile stillness of a held breath, but the deep, resonant quiet of a system in health. Arthur moved between them, a quiet conductor of two symphonies, his own resonance humming with a contented stability.

The change began subtly. Arthur felt it as a faint, crystalline prickle at the edge of his perception when he stepped through the Threshold. The Glimmerwood's eternal twilight seemed clearer, the colors of the leaves harder, as if being forged from light into gemstones.

The season turns, Fig communicated. *The First Frost approaches. It is not a weather of temperature, but of essence— a time of settling, of clarification.* The Frost will test it. It will seek out any weakness, any instability, and make it plain.

The following morning, he awoke in his own world to a

different kind of frost. A hard, white rime coated the garden, gripping the world with absolute cold. His father, seeing the frost, immediately clicked into engineer-mode. "The new plantings at the cut... Their roots are too shallow. They won't survive this if it lasts".

A parallel challenge: a Frostfall in the Glimmerwood, a killing frost in his own world.

"We'll need row covers," his father said, decisive. "It's a stopgap. But it might be enough".

An hour later, the three of them worked quickly at the railway cut, unrolling the fleecy fabric and anchoring them down with stones. It was a race against the deepening cold, a physical act of defense. As Arthur knelt, his fingers growing numb, he felt the connection thrum between his worlds. The act of protecting these physical seeds was an echo of his need to protect the Glimmerwood.

He focused his resonance not on the frost itself, but on the small, shielded space under the fabric. He hummed the complex harmony of protection and patience, willing the tiny roots to hold on. He felt a shift: the soil under his hands seemed to radiate a fraction more warmth. It was the Warden reinforcing the will to live.

In the Glimmerwood, the Frostfall deepened, clarifying the realm into a state of breathtaking, severe beauty. The leaves had not fallen, but transmuted into solid, intricate sculptures of light. The Frost was not an enemy. It was an archivist, Arthur realized.

He found a memory echo near the Vale of Echoed Songs—a complex weave of love, regret, and hope. The Frost sought to simplify it by attacking the hopeful strands, trying to reduce the memory to pure sorrow. Arthur's mission was to defend the complexity of the "bittersweet" state.

He poured his resonance into the vulnerable threads of hope, channeling a new energy: the resonance of protection from his own world. He wove the stubborn will to survive from the hidden seedlings into the memory's fabric, and the fragile filament of hope brightened, perfectly preserved. The two-way flow of the Balance was now a tangible tool.

On the fourth morning, snow began to fall, breaking the hard frost. The snow would insulate the ground, a reprieve. When Arthur stepped into the Glimmerwood, he felt the parallel shift. The severe, crystalline clarity was softening. The Frost was concluding its work. *We have passed the test,* Fig communicated. The Balance held. The new growth, in both worlds, has endured its first hardening.

CHAPTER TWENTY-SIX

THE DEEPENING COLD

The frost did not relinquish its grip. For three days, the world outside Arthur's window remained a study in monochrome, a landscape etched in glass and bone. The sun, when it appeared, was a pale, distant eye offering light but no warmth, its rays glancing off the frozen world without penetrating the deep cold that had settled in the soil and stone. Inside, the Pensive household developed its own rhythm to counter the siege. The heating hummed constantly, and the scent of soup and baking bread became a permanent, comforting presence, a sensory bulwark against the chill.

Their daily pilgrimage to the railway cut became a solemn ritual. Each morning, Arthur and his parents would trek through the brittle grass to check on their fledgling garden. The row covers, stiff with a permanent layer of rime, had become a symbol of their defiance. His father would meticulously inspect the anchors, his engineer's mind ensuring their temporary defense remained structurally sound. His mother would gently lift a corner of the fabric, her breath held, to check the soil beneath. It remained dark and unfrozen, a tiny, captured pocket of autumn held safe against the invading winter.

"They're holding," she would report each time, her voice filled with a quiet, fierce pride that Arthur knew transcended plants. It was about the project, the family, the shared act of preservation.

Arthur continued his work, his resonance a silent partner in their efforts. He wove threads of fortitude and resilience into the soil, a continuous, low-level hum of encouragement directed at the dormant seeds. He was not trying to make them grow; he was helping them remember how to wait, how to endure. He felt their tiny, latent lives huddled in the dark earth, and his own spirit huddled with them, a Warden standing watch over a kingdom of sleeping potential.

In the Glimmerwood, the Frostfall deepened, clarifying the realm into a state of breathtaking, severe beauty. The transformation was more profound than any Arthur had witnessed. The once-soft, sighing air was now so still and clear it felt sacred, a cathedral silence where every potential sound was held in perfect suspension. The bioluminescent moss had withdrawn its light completely, storing its energy deep within its core. The trees were the most changed. Their leaves of gold, violet, and silver had not fallen, but had transmuted. They were now solid, intricate sculptures of light, their inner luminescence frozen into permanent, glittering forms. To walk through the forest was to walk through a gallery of crystallized memories, each leaf a captured laugh, a fossilized tear, a moment of pure feeling made tangible and eternal.

The Frost was not an enemy, Arthur realized. It was an archivist. It was taking the vibrant, flowing energy of the Glimmerwood and turning it into a library of solid light, preserving the year's stories in a form that could survive the long, dreamless quiet to come. But the process was perilous. The clarifying power sought out every flaw, every unresolved emotion, and threatened to freeze it in its imperfect state.

He and Fig became patrolling guardians in the frozen gallery. Their task was not to stop the Frost, but to guide it, to ensure its clarifying power acted as a preservative, not a destructive force. They found echoes that were too complex, too tangled with conflicting emotions, and the Frost sought to simplify them by locking them in a single, dominant feeling.

They found one such echo near the Vale of Echoed Songs. It was a memory of a bittersweet parting—a complex weave of love, regret, and hope. The Frost was attacking the hopeful strands, trying to reduce the memory to pure sorrow. Arthur realized the Frost's cold logic saw "bittersweet" as unstable; it wanted the memory to be either "sweet" or "bitter" for structural integrity. His mission was to defend the complexity of the "bittersweet" state. Arthur and Fig worked in tandem. Fig, with its ancient wisdom, would gently reinforce the structure of the memory, holding its complex shape. Arthur, with his resonant empathy, would pour warmth into the vulnerable threads of hope and love, convincing the Frost that these, too, were essential parts of the story worth preserving. It was delicate, painstaking work, like restoring a priceless, frozen tapestry.

During one of these sessions, as Arthur focused on

reinforcing a filament of hope so thin it was almost invisible, he felt a new sensation. It was a faint, answering pulse from the direction of his own world. It was the resonance of the protected seeds under the row covers, their latent life strengthened by his constant attention. Their simple, stubborn will to survive was echoing back to him, a tiny but potent energy that he could channel. He wove this new thread into his work, and the fragile filament of hope in the bittersweet memory brightened, solidifying into the tapestry, perfectly preserved.

The two-way flow of the Balance was now a tangible tool. The Glimmerwood gave him the patterns, the understanding of memory and emotion. His own world gave him the raw, gritty strength of endurance, the stubborn will to live that was now fortifying the Glimmerwood against its own harsh season.

On the fourth morning, Arthur was woken not by his alarm, but by a change in the light. He went to the window. The killing frost was still there, but the sky was no longer a hard, featureless grey. It was a soft, uniform white, and fat, fluffy flakes of snow were beginning to drift down, slowly, peacefully, covering the sharp, glassy world in a soft, forgiving blanket.

Downstairs, his father was at the back door, holding it open and smiling. "Snow," he said, as if it were a victory. "The hard frost is breaking. The snow will insulate the ground. It's a reprieve."

At the railway cut, the transformation was magical. The harsh, white rime was being gentled by the falling snow. The row covers now looked like soft, sleeping forms under a fresh duvet. The terrible, penetrating cold was lifting, replaced by the muffled, peaceful quiet of a snowfall.

When Arthur stepped into the Glimmerwood that afternoon, he felt the parallel shift immediately. The severe, crystalline clarity of the Frostfall was softening. A gentle, shimmering haze filled the air, made of solidified light. The Frost was concluding its work. The realm was settling into its winter dream. The memories were preserved, the library was complete. The Glimmerwood was safe.

He found Fig waiting for him at the Heartwood. The great, braided trees were encased in a sheath of living diamond, their light pulsing slowly, deeply, in a rhythm of hibernation.

We have passed the test, Fig communicated, its own form looking more solid, more defined. The Balance held. The new growth, in both worlds, has endured its first hardening.

Arthur placed a hand on the frozen bark of the Heartwood. The double pulse was slower, but immensely powerful, like the heartbeat of a sleeping giant. He had done it. He had not just survived the Frost; he had learned from it, worked with it, and used the strength of one world to help the other. He was no longer just practicing the art of the Warden. He was mastering it.

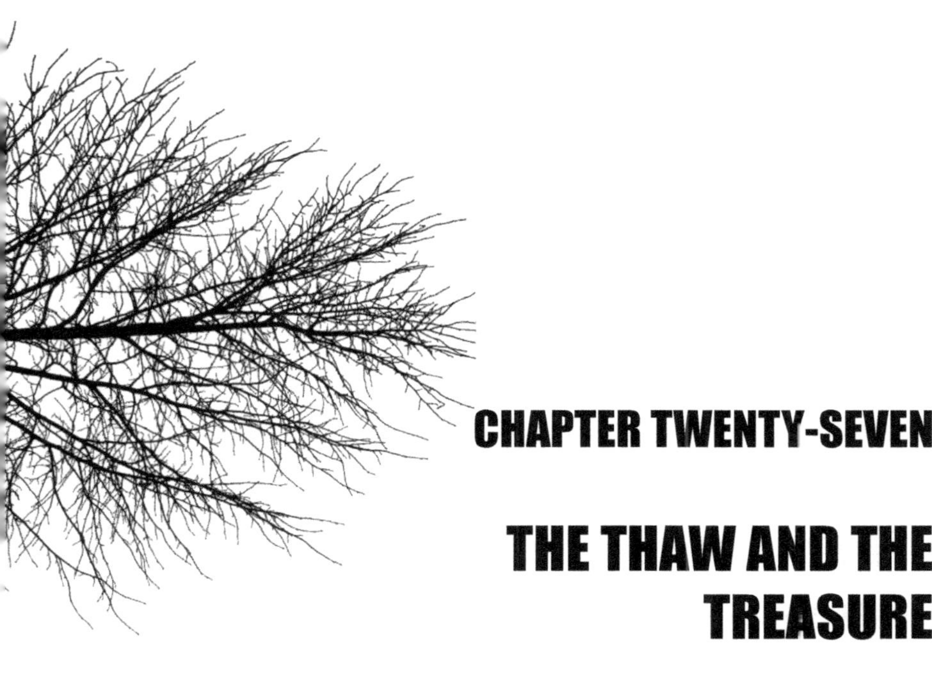

CHAPTER TWENTY-SEVEN

THE THAW AND THE TREASURE

The snow fell for a day and a night, a deep, hushing blanket that smoothed the world's sharp edges and ushered in a different, softer kind of cold. In Arthur's world, the killing frost was broken. The air still held a wintry bite, but the penetrating deep-freeze that threatened the roots of things had retreated. The railway cut, once a stark scar of white, was now a series of gentle, snowy hummocks, the row covers hidden from view but doing their work beneath the insulating layer. The crisis had passed, replaced by the patient, dormant quiet of true winter.

The thaw in the Glimmerwood was a more spectacular affair. It came not with dripping water or melting ice, but with a gradual softening of light. The severe, crystalline clarity of the Frostfall gave way to a gentle, internal luminescence. The trees, once like frozen sculptures, now seemed to breathe, their light pulsing in a slow, sleepy rhythm. The crystalline crust on the stream dissolved not into water, but into a mist of shimmering motes that rose and hung in the air, catching the soft light from the canopy and creating a permanent, gentle glitter in the atmosphere. The black, velvety moss began to show faint, tentative pulses of green deep within its core, like a distant star flickering to life.

The Frost had not just been a test; it had been a revelation. It had scoured the Glimmerwood clean, burning away the finest, most ephemeral echoes and clarifying the stronger ones, leaving the foundational structure of the realm exposed. And in that clarified state, something new—or rather, something very old—was revealed.

Arthur felt it as a low, persistent hum, a frequency far deeper and more solid than any memory-echo. It was a foundational note, the bass line upon which the Glimmerwood's symphony was built. It called to him not from the Weeping Grove or the Vale of Echoed Songs, but from a quiet, rocky slope where the trees grew thin and the quartz path faded into a scattering of pale stones.

He followed the hum, Fig gliding silently beside him, its own attention sharp with curiosity. *The Frost has uncovered something,* Fig communicated. *Something that was always here, but buried under the noise of countless smaller stories.*

They reached the slope. Now, Arthur could see the source of the hum. Partially embedded in the hillside, revealed where the Frost had lifted a layer of psychic sediment, was a Door. It was not made of wood or stone, but appeared woven from the gnarled, ancient roots of the Glimmerwood itself, twisted together into a perfect, arched shape. At its center was a lock, but it held no keyhole. Instead, there was a complex, interlocking pattern of runes that pulsed with the same deep, foundational hum.

"This wasn't here before," Arthur whispered, his breath catching. He reached out, but his hand stopped an inch from the root-bound surface. A powerful, gentle resistance pushed back, not a barrier of hostility, but one of profound significance. This was not a door to be forced.

It was always here, Fig corrected, its luminous eyes wide with awe. *The Frost did not create it. It revealed it. This is a Root-Lock. It is older than the Heartwood. It is a memory of the First Threshold.* It gestured to the runic pattern. *This is not a lock that accepts a metal key. It requires a key of understanding. A specific resonance.*

As Arthur stared at the pattern, the runes began to feel familiar. They were softer, more organic, like the veins on a leaf or the patterns of frost on a windowpane. They reminded him of the feeling-script in his grandfather's journal.

Nicholas, he thought, the realization dawning like the sun outside. *This is his. This is part of his legacy.*

He didn't have the key. Not yet. But the Frost, in its impartial work, had given him the map. It had shown him the door. The key, he knew with deep, instinctual certainty, was hidden in the other part of the legacy—the sketchbook and journal waiting for him at home.

The return to his own world was charged with a new, electric purpose. The winter quiet of the house was no longer just peaceful; it was pregnant with potential. He went straight to the attic, the familiar musty smell now like the scent of a treasure vault. He went directly to his grandfather's trunk.

He lifted out the leather-bound journal, the one filled with the feeling-script. Before, he had only deciphered fragments, overwhelmed by the emotional weight. Now, he had a focus. He laid it on the floor and opened it, not reading, but feeling. He let his resonance flow over the pages, not seeking a story, but searching for a pattern, a frequency that matched the deep, foundational hum of the Root-Lock.

He spent hours there, as the short winter day faded outside the circular window. He moved through sketches of the garden, maps of the "Quiet Country," and pages of dense, emotional script. And then, he found it. Not on a page of its own, but woven into the background of a beautiful, intricate drawing of the Twin Heartwoods.

In the negative space, drawn in the faintest lines of the feeling-script, was the exact same interlocking runic pattern from the Root-Lock.

As his resonance touched it, the page seemed to come alive. The pattern glowed with a soft, golden light, and a single, clear concept flowed into his mind, in a voice that was undeniably that of Nicholas Frost:

The Balance is not two, but three. The Remembering. The Forgetting. And the Foundation upon which they both stand. The First Story. The Warden is the keeper of all three. Find the

Foundation, Arthur.

It holds the answer to every question you have not yet learned to ask.

The glow faded. Arthur sat back, his mind reeling. The Root-Lock did not guard a place, but a story. The First Story. The Foundation of it all. His grandfather hadn't just been a Warden; he had been an explorer, a seeker of ultimate truths. And he was passing the quest on.

Arthur looked from the journal to the Key, warm in his pocket, and then out the window towards the Glimmerwood. The Frost had ended one challenge, but it had unveiled the greatest one yet. He was no longer just maintaining a Balance. He was being invited to understand its origin. The Warden's work was indeed never done. It was only ever beginning.

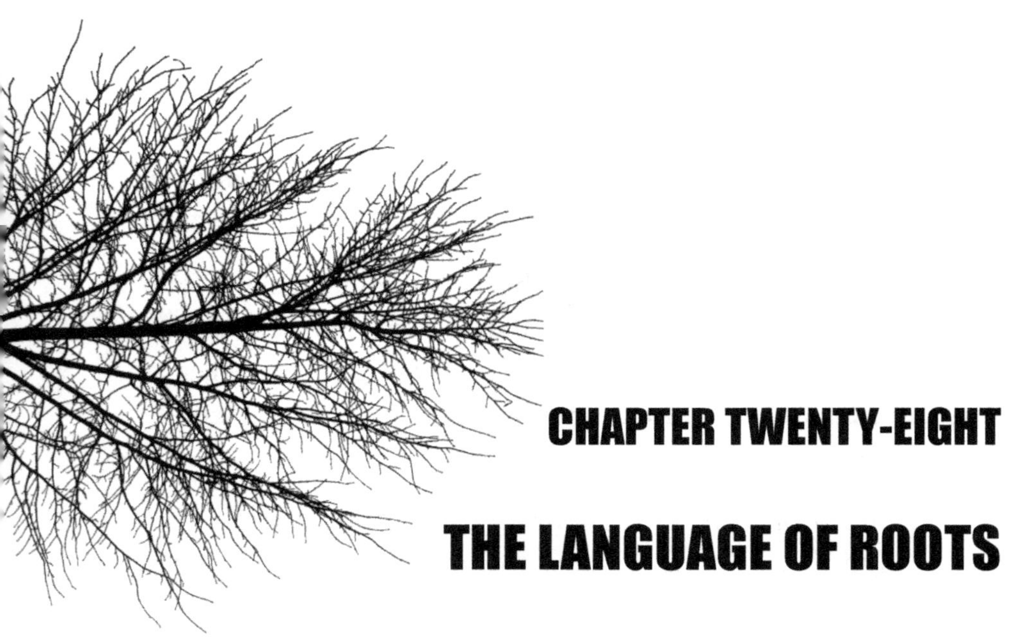

CHAPTER TWENTY-EIGHT

THE LANGUAGE OF ROOTS

The revelation of the Root-Lock settled into Arthur's soul not as a frantic call to action, but as a deep, resonant question that rewrote the map of his purpose. For so long, his role as Warden had been defined by reaction—to the Alchemist's silence, to the Memory-Seed's tyranny, to the Frost's clarifying harshness. Now, he was faced with a mystery that demanded not a reaction, but a profound, patient seeking. He was no longer a groundskeeper; he was an archaeologist of meaning, and the Root-Lock was the first, foundational dig site.

His first instinct—to rush back to the Glimmerwood and pour all his power against the ancient door—was resisted. The gentle, firm resistance he had felt was a teacher in itself. This was not a barrier to be broken, but a conversation to be joined. The key was understanding, and understanding could not be forced.

He began his work in the attic, treating his grandfather's journal as a sacred text. He would spend an hour on a single page, the one with the Root-Lock pattern woven into the Heartwoods. He would lay his hands upon the paper and pour his resonance into the drawn lines, not to activate them, but to listen. He was trying to hear the echo of the intention behind the ink, the specific frequency of his grandfather's wonder and frustration when he, too, had discovered this mystery.

It was slow, painstaking work. At first, he felt nothing but the familiar, warm hum of his grandfather's love. But as he persisted, sitting in the silent attic day after day, he began to detect finer notes within that hum. There was a tone of immense curiosity, a vibrant, golden thread of excitement. But woven through it was a darker, more somber strand—the feeling of a limit reached, a puzzle that had resisted even Nicholas Frost's profound understanding. His grandfather had not left him an answer; he had left him the same question, passed down like a family heirloom.

This solitary work in the attic began to change how he moved through his own world. The frantic energy of seeking was replaced by a deep, observational calm. At school, he found himself watching the patterns people made—how loneliness could create a silent, personal Frostfall around a person. He wasn't just seeing individuals anymore; he was seeing the foundational social structures, the root-locks of human interaction. He noticed how Liam Carter's aggression was a desperate, clumsy attempt to forge a connection, a distorted root trying to anchor itself. He saw how Anya's quiet art was her way of inscribing her own feeling-script onto the world.

At home, he watched his parents with this new, layered perception. He saw the deep, sturdy root-structure of their love, the way it had held fast even through years of quiet neglect. He saw the newer, more tender roots they were now growing towards him, and the old, petrified root of his grandfather's loss, now a monument integrated into their family's foundation. He was learning the language of roots by observing how they grew, tangled, and supported life in his own world.

After a week of this patient, internal preparation, he finally returned to the Glimmerwood. He went straight to the rocky slope, Fig a silent, approving presence at his side. The Root-Lock was as it was, the runes pulsing with their deep, slow hum. This time, Arthur did not approach it with a desire to open it. He sat before it, cross-legged on the cool, crystalline moss, as if in meditation.

He did not project his resonance at the lock. Instead, he let it settle within himself, tuning his own internal frequency to match the patient, observational state he had cultivated in the attic. He was not a key trying to fit a lock. He was a student making himself ready to receive a lesson.

For a long time, nothing happened. He simply sat, breathing in the clear, post-Frost air, feeling the immense, sleeping power of the Glimmerwood dreaming around him. He let his awareness expand, feeling the sturdy roots of the ancient trees, the deep, slow pulse of the Twin Heartwoods, the fragile, new growth of Gleam and the other minor echoes.

And then, as his own resonance achieved a state of perfect,

quiet receptivity, the Root-Lock responded. The interlocking runes didn't glow or shift. Instead, a single, pure note sounded in the depths of his mind. It was not a word, not a melody. It was a question. A feeling of profound, foundational inquiry.

What am I?

The question was not arrogant or demanding. It was open, patient, and ancient. It was the question the universe had asked at the moment of its creation. It was the question at the heart of every story, every memory, every act of forgetting.

Arthur knew, with a certainty that vibrated in his very bones, that an answer was not what was required. The key was not a solution, but the capacity to hold the question.

He sat there, contemplating the Root-Lock's foundational inquiry, not as a problem to be solved, but as a sacred object. He felt the lock's resonance settle around his own, acknowledging him. Recognizing a fellow seeker.

When he finally stood to leave, his body was stiff, but his spirit felt clearer than it ever had. He hadn't unlocked anything. But he had learned the first word of the language he needed to speak. He had learned to listen to the question.

CHAPTER TWENTY-NINE

THE UNWRITTEN PAGE

The silent communion with the Root-Lock did not provide Arthur with a sudden flash of insight or a magical password. Instead, it left him with a profound and humbling stillness, as if a great bell had been struck within him and he was now feeling the aftermath of its vibration—a deep, resonant quiet that clarified his thoughts and sharpened his senses. The question— *What am I?*—echoed in the chambers of his mind not as a demand, but as a lens through which he now viewed everything.

This new, contemplative state transformed his daily life into a continuous act of research. His walks to and from school were no longer a gauntlet to be run, but a living library of foundational behaviors. He observed the old stone wall settled into the earth, its mossy stones a testament to a long, patient conversation with gravity. He saw the intricate, desperate root-lock of a teenage romance unfolding by the bike sheds—a clumsy, passionate attempt to answer the question of identity through another person. He watched the barista perform the same ritual with the espresso machine daily, each repetition a tiny root of habit anchoring her in the flow of time. He wasn't merely seeing things; he was reading the world as a vast, interconnected text written in the language of roots and patterns.

This shift in perception was most powerful at home. Dinner conversations were no longer just exchanges of information. He listened to the underlying structures. He heard the sturdy, old-growth root of his parents' shared history in the way they could communicate an entire thought with a glance. He heard the new, green shoot of their rekindled connection to him in the questions they asked, questions that now sought true understanding, not polite noise. The petrified root of his grandfather's memory was clearly visible, not as a scar, but as a load-bearing pillar in the architecture of their family. He began to understand that the Root-Lock's question was not asking for a singular, cosmic answer. It was asking how any single thing—a person, a family, a memory—came to be itself, and how that self was inextricably woven into the tapestry of everything else.

He brought this refined awareness back to his grandfather's journal. He understood the page with the Root-Lock pattern was the destination, and he needed to trace the path his grandfather had walked to get there. He began again from the beginning, but this time, he was searching for patterns of thought, for the intellectual and spiritual roots of Nicholas Frost's own understanding.

He spent days this way, the winter darkness closing in

outside the attic window. He followed his grandfather's journey from the first, awestruck maps, through the complex charts of the "Quiet Country," to the philosophical musings in the feeling-script. He felt Nicholas's initial joy, his frustration with the Alchemist's early incursions, and his dawning understanding of the Balance. It was like walking a well-trodden path behind a guide, seeing the same landmarks he himself had seen.

And then, he found the gap.

It was near the end of the journal. The entries were filled with a new, intense focus. The feeling-script was tighter, thrumming with a frequency of deep, almost obsessive concentration. Nicholas was clearly on the trail of the Root-Lock. There were sketches of the runic pattern, notes that felt like theoretical calculations of resonance. Then, abruptly, the nature of the entries changed.

The complex script gave way to simpler, more fundamental feelings. There were pages that held nothing but the sensation of deep, earthy patience, like a root growing in slow motion. Another page was imbued with the pure, clear frequency of a single, sustained musical note. It was as if Nicholas had realized that complex understanding was not the key, and had begun to deconstruct his own knowledge, returning to the most basic, foundational elements of existence.

The final written entry was not a feeling, but a simple, drawn symbol in normal ink. It was a circle, divided not into two, but three equal, interlocking segments. In one segment was a small, stylized leaf. In another, a wisp of smoke or mist. In the third, a single, unadorned dot. Beneath it, in shaky, physical handwriting, were the words: *The Trinity is the Key. And the door is not a door.*

And then, the last page of the journal was... blank.

It wasn't that it had been left unused. Arthur could feel the difference. The rest of the journal hummed with the accumulated energy of his grandfather's life and work. This page was different. It held a potential. A silence. But it was a charged silence, the kind that exists in the moment after a question is asked and before the answer is given. He laid his hand on the blank page, and a single, clear concept flowed into him, the last thing his grandfather had imprinted there: *Your turn.*

The message was unmistakable. Nicholas Frost had reached the limit of his own journey. He had deduced the nature of the key—this "Trinity"—and understood the paradoxical nature of the "door." But he had not been able to take the final step. He had run out of time, or perhaps lacked a specific quality of resonance that Arthur possessed. He had prepared the ground, and now he was passing the seeds to his grandson.

Arthur closed the journal, his heart pounding. He wasn't just solving his grandfather's mystery. He was continuing his work. The blank page was an invitation, a challenge, and a declaration of faith all at once.

He now had the final clues: The key was a Trinity. And the Root-Lock was not a door in the conventional sense. He thought of the gentle, firm resistance, not a barrier but a presence. He thought of the question it had asked. *What am I?*

A door was a passage. But what if the Root-Lock wasn't a passage? What if it was a... mirror? A point of reflection? What if unlocking it wasn't about going somewhere else, but about understanding the place you were already in, on a deeper level?

The pieces were beginning to shift and align in his mind, not yet forming a complete picture, but the outline was there. He needed to understand this Trinity. Leaf, Mist, Dot. Remembering, Forgetting, and... Foundation? It felt right, but it was still an intellectual concept. He needed to feel it. He needed to find it not in a book, but in the living world.

He stood, the blank page of the journal seared into his memory. The path was clear. The theoretical work was over. It was time to go back into the world, both of them, and seek the living expression of this Trinity. The final leg of the journey had begun.

CHAPTER THIRTY

THE TRINITY IN THE WORLD

The symbols from his grandfather's journal—the Leaf, the Mist, the Dot—became a constant, rotating triptych in Arthur's mind. They were no longer mere drawings; they were focal points for his newly-honed perception, each one a profound question. He understood now that the key wasn't a physical object or a secret phrase, but a state of understanding, a resonance that could only be achieved by internalizing these fundamental principles. The blank page at the end of the journal was his canvas, and his life was the paint. He had to find the Trinity alive in the world around him.

He started with the Leaf. It was the easiest to grasp, the most immediately present. The Leaf represented growth, memory, and connection—it was the Remembering. He saw it everywhere: in the intricate, vein-like patterns of frost on his windowpane each morning, each one a unique, crystalline memory of the night's cold. He saw it in the family tree his mother had drawn in the photo album, its branches representing their sprawling, interconnected lineage. He felt it most strongly in the Glimmerwood—in every shimmering echo, in the very leaves that were captured memories. The Leaf was life, story, and the past woven into the present. He spent days absorbing this concept, walking through the frozen park and seeing not dead branches, but a million Leaf-memories sleeping, waiting for the sun to ask them to remember how to be green again.

Next, he turned his attention to the Mist. This was harder. The Mist was the opposite of the Leaf's solid, defined presence. It was the Forgetting. It was release, ambiguity, and the space between things. He found it in the steam rising from his cup of tea, a form that was there and not there, constantly dissolving and reforming. He heard it in the white noise of the shower, a sound that erased all others, creating a blank slate. He felt it most powerfully one afternoon when a dense fog rolled in from the river, swallowing the world outside his window. The world vanished into a soft, grey nothingness. It wasn't frightening; it was peaceful. The fog wasn't destroying the world; it was simply reminding him that reality wasn't as solid and permanent as it seemed. It was the Alchemist's work, but gentle, natural. The Mist was the necessary erasure that made the Leaf's clarity possible. It was the deep breath between thoughts.

But the Dot... the Dot eluded him. It was the third part of the Trinity, the Foundation. It was not the Remembering, nor the Forgetting. It had to be the thing upon which they both depended. He stared at the symbol—a simple, unadorned point. It represented a location, a moment, a source. He tried to find it in the center of things, but these felt like interpretations, not experiences. The Dot had to be something else entirely.

His frustration grew. He had grasped the Leaf and the Mist. He could feel their resonances, understand their roles in the great Balance. But without the Dot, the Trinity was incomplete. It was a bridge with no central pier, destined to collapse.

The breakthrough came from an unexpected source: his father. The project at the railway cut was in its winter dormancy, but the planning continued. One evening, his father called him over to his tablet. He had created a new, three-dimensional model of the entire cut.

"Look," his father said, his voice filled with a quiet excitement Arthur hadn't heard in years. He zoomed in on the model. "I've been thinking about the Foundation. Not the terraces, but what's underneath." The model became transparent, revealing a complex, layered diagram beneath the soil. "There's the topsoil we amended. Then the older, compacted subsoil. But here," he pointed to a single, central point deep in the digital earth, "is the bedrock. It's what everything else rests on. It doesn't grow. It doesn't change. It doesn't care what we plant on the surface. It simply is. It's the foundation. Without understanding its level, its composition, any structure we build on top is inherently unstable."

Arthur stared at the screen, at the digital representation of the bedrock, a single, fixed point in the virtual landscape. The Dot.

It wasn't a thing you could hold. It wasn't a memory or an act of forgetting. It was a state of being. The Is-ness. The point of pure existence before it became anything in particular. The Dot was the moment before the seed was a Leaf, before the water became Mist. It was the First Story his grandfather had written of—not a story with a plot, but the story of Existence itself asserting "I Am."

The understanding didn't arrive as a thought, but as a shift in his entire being. It was a resonance so deep and fundamental it had been humming in the background of his soul his entire life, the baseline frequency of his own existence. He had been trying to find the Dot outside of himself, when it was the very core of what he was. The Root-Lock's question—*What am I?* —was the Dot asking about itself.

He didn't need to go to the Glimmerwood to test this. He sat on the floor of his room, closed his eyes, and turned his awareness inward. He let go of the Leaf-memories of his day, of the Mist-like worries about the future. He pushed past the stories of being Arthur Pensive, the Warden, the grandson. He sought the silent, unwavering point of consciousness at the center of it all, the witness that was aware of the memories and the forgetting but was not defined by them.

And he found it. A point of pure, silent awareness. The Dot. The Foundation.

He held that feeling, that resonance of being the foundational witness. Then, gently, he brought the Leaf into his awareness—the memory of his mother's smile that morning. He didn't get lost in the memory; he simply observed it arising within the space of the Dot. Then, he brought in the Mist—the feeling of releasing a minor worry about a school assignment. He observed that, too, as it dissolved back into the space from which it came.

Leaf, Mist, Dot. Remembering, Forgetting, and the foundational Awareness that held them both. He had done it.

He hadn't just understood the Trinity intellectually. He had become it.

He stood up, his body feeling both incredibly light and immensely solid. He didn't need to rush to the Root-Lock. He knew, with a certainty that surpassed knowledge, that he was ready. He had found the key. It had been inside him all along. The journey to the Glimmerwood now would not be an attempt to unlock something, but an act of sharing what he had discovered. He was not going to open a door. He was going to introduce himself.

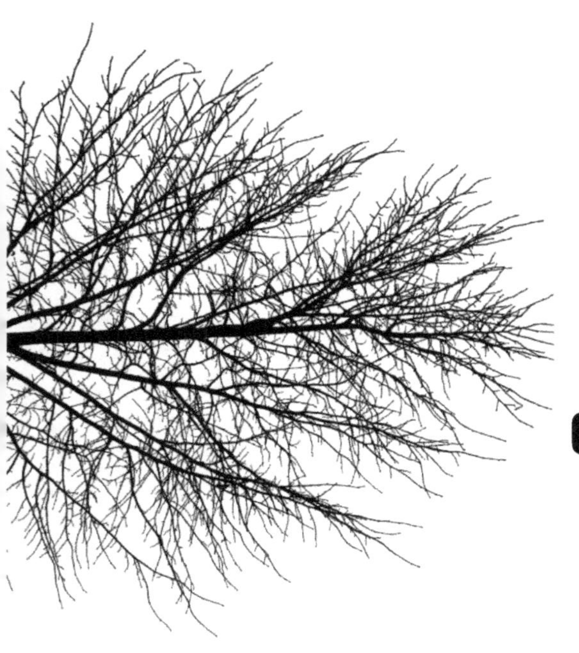

CHAPTER THIRTY-ONE

THE CONVERSATION AT THE ROOT

A profound and unshakable calm settled over Arthur as he prepared to return to the Glimmerwood. This was not the tense stillness before a battle, nor the frantic hope of a final attempt. It was the deep, resonant quiet of a journey reaching its natural destination. He did not rush. He walked through his own garden, his hand brushing against the frost-rimed hawthorn branches, feeling the Leaf-potential sleeping within. He breathed in the crisp, cold air, watching his breath mist before him, feeling the gentle embrace of the Mist, the great, soft eraser of the world. And beneath it all, he felt the Dot—the unwavering, foundational awareness that was him, Arthur Pensive, observing it all.

When he stepped through the Threshold, the Glimmerwood felt different because he was different. He did not see a realm of magic separate from himself, but an external expression of the same principles he had just discovered within. The crystallized memories on the trees were the Leaf, made beautiful and permanent by the Frost. The shimmering, clear air was the Mist, clarified and serene. And the deep, humming pulse of the Heartwoods was the Dot, the foundational "I Am" of this entire world. He was not a visitor here. He was a part of its Trinity.

Fig was waiting for him on the quartz path, but the creature did not need to ask any questions. It took one look at Arthur, at the new, settled depth in his eyes, the way his resonance no longer probed the world but simply was a part of it, and a feeling of immense, timeless completion flowed from it.

You are ready, Fig communicated, and the thought was not one of guidance, but of welcome. The Root-Lock has been waiting for you.

They walked to the rocky slope in a silence that was more eloquent than any conversation. The Glimmerwood itself seemed to be holding its breath, the gentle murmur of echoes stilled in anticipation. The Root-Lock stood as it had before, the ancient, root-woven door with its pulsing, runic pattern. But Arthur no longer saw it as a barrier. He saw it as a face. The face of the Glimmerwood's deepest self.

He did not approach it with his hands outstretched, nor did he sit before it in meditation. He simply walked up to it and stood, present and open. He was not there to do anything. He was there to be.

He allowed the three resonances within him to find their

natural balance. He did not force them. He simply became aware of them, as one becomes aware of breathing.

First, the Dot. The core of his own awareness, the silent witness. He felt its solid, unwavering presence, the simple, profound fact of his own existence. This was the Foundation. The "I Am."

Then, from that still center, arose the Leaf. He felt the memory of his entire journey—the loneliness, the discovery, the fear, the friendship with Fig, the reconciliation with his parents, the quiet triumphs and the profound lessons. He felt the memory of his grandfather, Nicholas Frost, not as a ghost, but as a living thread in the tapestry of his own being. This was the Remembering. The story.

And finally, the Mist. He felt the release of all of it. He let go of the need for the journey to be anything other than what it was. He released the identity of "the Warden" as a title to be upheld. He allowed the specific details of the memories to soften at the edges, not forgotten, but held lightly, their sharpness dissolved in the understanding that they were patterns dancing on the surface of the deep, still Dot. This was the Forgetting. The release.

He held this state—Dot, Leaf, Mist. Foundation, Remembering, Forgetting. Being, Story, Release. He held them not as separate parts, but as a single, integrated whole. A Trinity.

He did not project this resonance at the lock. He simply allowed it to be his state of being.

The Root-Lock responded.

The runes did not flash or rearrange themselves. Instead, the entire door, woven from the living roots of the Glimmerwood, began to relax. The roots, which had been twisted tightly together for eons, began to soften and unfurl. They did not break or snap; they unfurled, slowly and gracefully, like a flower opening to the sun. There was no sound of grinding stone or shattering magic, only the soft, rustling whisper of ancient wood moving for the first time in centuries.

Where the door had been, an opening appeared. But it was not a doorway leading to a hidden chamber or a new world. It was an opening that revealed... more of the same. It was a deeper view into the rocky slope, as if a layer of illusion had been gently pulled aside. There was no treasure chest, no glowing artifact, no secret library.

There was only a single, simple thing.

Set into a niche in the exposed earth, nestled amongst the very roots of the Glimmerwood, was a stone. It was smooth and grey, about the size of his palm, and perfectly oval. It was utterly ordinary. It was, in fact, identical in every way to the smooth, grey stone he carried in his pocket, the one he had always considered his anchor, the first and most cherished item in his collection of quiet things.

A wave of understanding, so vast and so simple it was almost dizzying, washed over him. The First Story was not a narrative. It was the story of a single, foundational act: the act of noticing. The act of a consciousness—a Dot—becoming aware of another. Of a universe becoming aware of itself through the first, simple act of attention. The stone was the first "other." The first thing that was not the self. The entire Glimmerwood, with all its complex echoes and memories, was just an elaborate, beautiful retelling of that first, primal moment when existence said, "I Am," and then, in the very next instant, noticed a stone and said, "And you are too."

The Root-Lock had not been guarding a secret. It had been guarding a mirror. And in that mirror, Arthur saw the most profound truth of all: he was not the Warden of the Glimmerwood. He was the Glimmerwood. He was a localized expression of the same foundational awareness that had noticed the first stone. So was his grandfather. So was Fig. So was every person in his own world. The lock was not a lock. It was a teacher. And the lesson was complete.

He reached into the niche and picked up the stone. It was warm. It hummed with the same foundational frequency as the one in his pocket, as his own heart, as the Glimmerwood itself. It was not a reward. It was a reminder.

He turned to Fig. The Echo-Folk was glowing with a soft, golden light, its form more real and present than ever before. There were no words, no thoughts exchanged. The understanding was absolute and shared.

Arthur Pensive turned and walked away from the Root-Lock, the second smooth, grey stone held gently in his hand. He did not look back. There was no need. The door was open because he had realized there had never been a door at all. There was only ever the conversation. And he was now a fluent speaker.

CHAPTER THIRTY-TWO

THE INTEGRATION

The transition back was not a transition between worlds, but a gentle shifting of focus within a single, unified reality. Arthur walked back through the Threshold into his own garden, the two smooth, grey stones—one from his pocket, one from the Root-Lock niche—a comfortable, balanced weight in his hands. The winter air was sharp in his lungs, the skeletal branches of the hawthorn tree a stark lattice against the twilight sky. But he no longer saw a separation. The tree was not just a tree; it was a Glimmerwood echo of patience, a Leaf-memory of summer held in the Mist of winter, all resting on the Dot-foundation of its essential tree-ness. The world had not changed; his perception of it had been irrevocably deepened.

He did not go to the attic. He went into the living room. His mother was on the sofa, the completed photo album open on her lap. His father was in his armchair, simply looking at the pocket watch on the mantelpiece. The scene was a perfect, living tableau of the Trinity. The album was the Leaf, heavy with remembered stories. The watch was the Mist, a monument to loss softened by time and acceptance into a peaceful presence. And the quiet, shared space between them was the Dot, the foundational love that required no story, no memory, to simply be.

They looked up as he entered. Words would have been clumsy, insufficient tools for the truth he now carried. Instead, he walked to the coffee table and gently set the two identical grey stones side-by-side on its worn, wooden surface.

He looked at his parents, and he simply let the understanding within him resonate, not as a projected force, but as his natural state of being. He was not hiding a secret life anymore; he was sharing his whole self.

His mother's eyes moved from the stones to his face. Her gaze, usually sharp and analytical, softened with a deep, intuitive recognition. She didn't see two rocks. She saw a statement. A completion. She smiled, a slow, warm smile that held no questions, only acceptance.

His father followed her gaze. The man who had been gently tending the petrified root of his own grief saw something else. He saw symmetry. He saw balance. He saw a quiet answer to a question he had never known how to ask. He gave a single, slow nod, his eyes meeting Arthur's with a depth of understanding that transcended generations.

In that silent exchange, the last vestiges of the old, lonely house dissolved. The Pensive household was now fully integrated, not just as a family, but as a conscious part of the great, humming Balance of all things. Arthur was home, truly and completely.

The following days were a practice in this new, integrated awareness. He went to school, and the chaotic symphony of the hallways was no longer a noise to be endured, but a vibrant, if sometimes dissonant, expression of the same principles. He saw the Leaf in the cliques and friendships. He saw the Mist in the way gossip flared and died, in the anxieties that were felt and then released. And beneath it all, in every single person, he could now sense the Dot—the silent, often frightened, but always present core of pure being.

He felt a profound compassion for Liam Carter, whose aggressive bluster was a distorted Leaf, a story of toughness shouted to cover a Dot that felt small and unseen. Arthur met his eyes and offered a simple, neutral nod, an acknowledgment of his existence that held no judgment, no fear. Liam, for the first time, looked confused, then thoughtful, before turning away without a snide comment. A tiny root of a different story had been planted.

His friendship with Anya deepened into a silent, powerful bond. She began a new drawing, not of dragons or phoenixes, but of two identical stones resting at the roots of a great, braided tree. She gave it to him without a word. He accepted it without thanks. They were both speaking the same language now, the language of the Root.

In the Glimmerwood, his role transformed entirely. He was a presence that was. His walks with Fig were now shared contemplations. Arthur's integrated resonance—the living

Trinity within him—acted as a stabilizing force for the entire realm. The Echo-Folk, especially the newer ones like Gleam, were drawn to him for the calm, foundational certainty he radiated. The Glimmerwood, in response, grew in a profound, settled peace. The Balance was no longer a dynamic state to be maintained; it was the natural condition of a system that had become fully conscious of itself.

He visited the Root-Lock often. The roots remained unfurled, the opening clear. It was a place of remembrance, a quiet grove where he would go to sit and simply feel the truth of what he was. It was his sanctuary, because it was the place that most perfectly reflected the world's—and his own—true nature.

One such afternoon, as he sat in the root-grove, he felt a familiar, warm resonance approaching. It was softer, woven with threads of intellectual curiosity and a deep, burgeoning love. A moment later, his mother stepped through the Threshold.

She stood for a long moment, her hand still on the bark of the oak tree, her eyes wide, taking in the Glimmerwood. She simply absorbed it, her historian's soul recognizing a truth more profound than any she had ever studied in a book. Her gaze moved from the crystallized trees to the shimmering stream, and finally to Arthur, sitting peacefully amidst the unfurled roots.

She walked towards him, her steps slow and reverent. She looked at the open Root-Lock, at the niche where the stone had been, and then at Arthur's face.

"It's all true, isn't it?" she whispered, her voice full of wonder. "The maps. The stories. The quiet things."

Arthur smiled. "It's all true," he said softly. "And it always has been."

She sat beside him on the soft moss, and together, mother and son sat in the heart of the mystery, not as explorers, but as natives returned home. The Warden's work was complete. The work of being had just begun.

CHAPTER THIRTY-THREE

THE UNSPOKEN UNDERSTANDING

The silent communion in the root-grove between Arthur and his mother was a threshold crossed, not with a fanfare, but with the soft, definitive click of a final piece settling into its destined place. Eleanor Pensive did not emerge from the Glimmerwood with frantic questions. She carried its truth within her like a warm, heavy stone, a secret knowledge that changed the color and texture of everything in her own world.

The change in the Pensive household deepened, becoming as fundamental as the shifting of seasons. Eleanor began to cultivate her own quietness. She started taking walks in the garden, her hand resting on the old oak not in curiosity, but in recognition. She was listening.

Her scholarship found a new, living subject. She began a new private journal, not of feeling-script, but a record of patterns. She sketched the Fibonacci spiral of a pinecone and the fractal repetition of frost on the windowpane. In the margin next to the leaf veins, she wrote: *"The pattern of growth is the pattern of decay, perfectly balanced in complexity"*. She was documenting the grammar of the Leaf in her own world, finding the Glimmerwood's fingerprints everywhere.

Alistair, in his own way, was undergoing a parallel transformation. He understood systems and foundations. The rich stillness of the house now replaced the old tense quiet. His response was to build. The railway cut project became his meditation. He began studying mycology, learning about the vast, hidden network of mycelium—the Dot of the forest. He started introducing beneficial fungi to the soil, understanding, on a gut level, that he was tending to the Foundation.

Arthur watched this beautiful, unorchestrated symphony unfold. His family was harmonizing with the Balance, each in their own unique key, without him needing to conduct them. He was the still point in their turning world, the Dot around which their Leaf-stories and Mist-releases could dance freely.

This integration extended to Arthur's life at school. The neutral acknowledgment he had offered Liam Carter had, over weeks, eroded Liam's hostility. One day, Liam approached Arthur in the library. "That girl. Anya. The one who draws," Liam mumbled. "Her stuff's... it's good".

It was a tiny interaction, but to Arthur, it was a seismic shift. Liam's aggression had been a Mist. He was now, tentatively, trying to grow a Leaf—an identity connected to something positive. Arthur had done nothing but be a steady Dot in his landscape, and that simple, unwavering presence had created enough stability for a new, fragile thing to take root.

Arthur was the awareness in the noise, the stillness in the pain, the clarity in the confusion. He was the Warden, not of a place, but of a state of being. And his ward was everywhere.

CHAPTER THIRTY-FOUR

THE GREAT AWAKENING

Winter's grip did not break dramatically, but softened day by day, like a great beast slowly uncurling from its long sleep. The deep, hard frosts became less frequent. During the day, the sun gained strength, warming the world, coaxing the memory of green from the frozen earth. Arthur felt the change as a slow, rising tide in both his worlds, a resonant hum of anticipation that grew with every passing day.

In the Glimmerwood, the Great Awakening was a spectacle of pure, resonant joy. The crystalline sheath that had encased the realm during the Frostfall began, not to melt, but to sublimate. The frozen memories on the trees and the glittering mist dissolved directly from solid light back into vibrant, flowing energy. It was not a thaw, but a reanimation. The forest, which had been a silent, crystalline library, became a living symphony once more. The stream's song, which had held that thread of anticipation, now burst forth in a triumphant, gushing melody. The bioluminescent moss pulsed with a fierce, emerald radiance.

The memory-echoes themselves seemed to stretch and sigh, their colors deepening, their forms becoming more complex and nuanced. Arthur and Fig walked through the realm, their very presence a catalyst. Arthur's integrated Trinity—his Dot-awareness, his Leaf-memories, his Mist-release—acted as a tuning fork for the awakening forest. Echoes that had been simple shimmers now unfolded into intricate, short-lived tableaus. The Glimmerwood was not just remembering; it was re-membering, pulling itself back together with more detail and vitality than ever before.

Fig was in its element, a master gardener tending a field of exploding life. Gleam and the other younger Echo-Folk followed in its wake, learning the art of nurturing this surge of returning energy. The Balance was not just restored; it was vibrant, dynamic, overflowing with the pent-up potential of its long dormancy.

In Arthur's world, the parallel Awakening was quieter, messier, and just as beautiful. The snow receded from the railway cut. The day the temperature crept reliably above freezing, the three Pensives gathered there for the unveiling. There was a ceremonial feeling to it, a shared held breath as Alistair and Arthur carefully rolled back the fleecy fabric.

The earth beneath was dark, rich, and alive. And there, scattered across the terraces like tiny, green promises, were the seedlings. The Lupine had pushed up their first, fern-like leaves. The Columbine showed delicate, rounded cotyledons. They were small, vulnerable, and utterly triumphant.

Eleanor knelt, her fingers gently brushing a Lupine seedling. "They remembered," she whispered, her voice thick with emotion.

Alistair stood with his hands on his hips. "The foundation held," he said, his engineer's assessment carrying a deeper meaning. "The structure was sound."

Arthur felt the connection thrum between the cut and the Glimmerwood. The green shoots were the Leaf, the manifest memory of the seeds they had planted. The rolled-back covers were the Mist, the release of their protective struggle. And the rich, living soil was the Dot, the foundational potential from which it all sprang. He placed his two grey stones at the base of the first terrace, a small, personal monument to the Trinity that had made this possible.

This act of creation, of witnessing the literal fruits of their labor, solidified the new dynamic of their family. Evenings were now often spent planning the next phase of the cut. Alistair talked of companion planting and natural pest control, his blueprints replaced by botanical guides. Eleanor researched the folklore of their chosen plants, adding a layer of story to the soil. Arthur listened, his resonance quietly reinforcing their shared purpose, feeling their individual energies weaving together into a stronger, collective root structure.

The change was evident at school, too. Spring seemed to loosen something in the student body. Anya's art show was a quiet success. Arthur saw Liam Carter lurking at the back of the crowd, looking intently at the drawing of the two stones at the rooted tree. It was a start.

Arthur himself felt a new sense of belonging. He was no longer the invisible boy. People started to come to him, not with their problems, but just to talk. They felt the calm, steady Dot-presence in him and were unconsciously drawn to it.

One warm, Saturday afternoon in late spring, Arthur took his mother to the Glimmerwood. They stepped through the Threshold into a realm riotous with life and light. Eleanor stood speechless, tears in her eyes, as a shimmer of pure, golden joy—an echo of a long-forgotten wedding day—drifted past them.

They found Fig and Gleam by the stream. Fig communicated a feeling of welcome so warm it felt like a physical embrace. As they stood there, a family of echoes of deer emerged from the trees and drank from the stream. It was a scene of such profound peace and beauty that it felt like a blessing.

Eleanor turned to Arthur, her face illuminated by the Glimmerwood's light. "This is what he was trying to protect," she said, her voice full of awe. "Your grandfather. This... this aliveness."

Arthur nodded. "Not just protect," he said. "To understand it. To become a part of it."

And he knew, looking at his mother's face, that the legacy of Nicholas Frost was secure. It was no longer a secret to be kept, but a truth to be lived. The Great Awakening was not just happening in the Glimmerwood and the railway cut; it was happening in their hearts. The long winter was over. The world was awake, and so were they.

CHAPTER THIRTY-FIVE

THE STEADY STATE

The vibrant explosion of spring settled, as all things must, into the steady, humming rhythm of early summer. The Great Awakening had not been a fleeting moment, but a transition into a new, elevated state of being for both of Arthur's worlds. The frantic energy of growth softened into the deep, confident pulse of life in full bloom. Arthur himself moved through this new reality with a sense of belonging so complete it felt like he had been grafted into the very fabric of existence. The loneliness that had once been his defining feature was now a distant memory, a fossil from a previous geological age of his soul.

The railway cut was no longer a project; it was a landmark. The Lupine stood in tall, majestic spires of purple and blue. The Columbine nodded their delicate, bell-like flowers, and the Yarrow formed a soft, feathery carpet of white blooms. The cut had been woven back into the town's story, a new chapter of reclamation and beauty. Arthur's family continued to tend it, but the work was no longer about defense or restoration. It was about stewardship, a gentle pruning here, a new planting there, a joyful participation in a cycle that was now self-sustaining.

This tangible success in the human world had a profound effect on Alistair Pensive. The man who had once found his satisfaction in the sterile precision of blueprints now found a deeper pleasure in the unpredictable grace of a blooming flower. He started a small compost bin, fascinated by the process of decay transforming into new life—the ultimate expression of the Mist giving way to the Leaf. Arthur could feel the understanding in him, a resonant harmony with the principles of the Balance.

One evening, Alistair presented Arthur with a small, beautifully crafted wooden box. Inside, nestled on a bed of velvet, was the silver pocket watch.

"It's still stopped," his father said, his voice quiet. "But it doesn't have to be hidden away. I thought... you might understand it better than I do."

It was the most significant gesture of trust Arthur had ever received. The watch was no longer a symbol of frozen grief, but a shared heirloom, a Leaf-memory of Nicholas that they could now hold lightly, without the crushing weight of the Mist of sorrow. Arthur accepted it, the cool metal a comforting weight in his palm. He understood its perfect, stopped nature was part of its story.

Arthur walked to the coffee table where the two Root-

Lock stones rested and gently placed the silver watch beside them. The sight of the three artifacts—two Dots of existence and a Leaf of time frozen in place—created a profound, visible statement of integrated family history.

In the Glimmerwood, the realm had achieved a state of harmony Arthur had never before witnessed. The Echo-Folk, led by Fig and the now-confident Gleam, moved through the forest as conscious curators of the memory-echoes. The Alchemist's function was understood and integrated. Arthur would sometimes see a patch of grey, pleasant silence where faint echoes had gently been allowed to fade, making space for new, more vibrant memories to form. The Mist was performing its necessary work with the gentle precision of a falling leaf. The Balance was not a tense truce, but a collaborative dance.

Arthur's visits were now less about patrols and more about communion. He would often find a sun-dappled spot and simply sit. He was like a stone in a river, the flow of memories and energies moving around and through him. His presence, his steady Dot-awareness, acted as a grounding point for the entire realm. Echo-Folk would sometimes drift near him just to bask in the calm he radiated.

It was during one of these visits that Fig led him to a new development. In a quiet clearing, a new structure was growing. Saplings were weaving themselves together to form the walls and roof of a small, intimate bower. A bench of living wood was slowly taking shape.

"It is for you," Fig communicated, its thought-voice filled with deep, settled joy. "A place for the Warden to simply... be.

A root-grove of your own."

Arthur was overwhelmed. This was the Glimmerwood's way of saying he was home. The bower was a physical manifestation of his integrated role. He sat on the nascent bench and felt a sense of arrival so profound it brought tears to his eyes.

This deep integration expressed itself in subtle, new abilities. He found he no longer needed to physically be in the Glimmerwood to sense its state. The Threshold was becoming less of a door and more of a permeable membrane in his own consciousness. He also found he could, with intense focus, sense the foundational state of people around him. He could feel the quality of their Dot. It wasn't intrusive; it was empathetic. It allowed him to meet people where they were, to offer the simple, steady presence of his own calm when it was needed.

He was no longer Arthur Pensive, the boy who visited a magic forest. He was Arthur Pensive, the living bridge. The human expression of the Glimmerwood's heart. The embodiment of the Balance in a world that often forgot it existed.

One evening, as he sat on the finished bench in his bower, Fig settled beside him. "The work changes," Fig communicated. "It becomes not a doing, but a state. You have learned the final lesson."

Arthur nodded. "It's not about fixing things anymore, is it? It's about belonging to them."

"Yes," Fig's thought was a soft sigh of agreement. "To belong to a thing is to love it. And to love a thing is to understand it. And to understand a thing is to be its Warden, naturally and without effort."

They sat in silence for a long time, two friends, two guardians, two pieces of a single, breathing whole. The symphony of the Glimmerwood played around them, and Arthur was no longer just a listener or a conductor. He was the silence between the notes, the space that held the music, the awareness that made the song possible.

The Steady State was not an ending. It was a beginning that would last forever.

EPILOGUE

THE QUIET DISSONANCE

The balance held. It was a perfect equilibrium, tended not by magic wands, but by a quiet presence and a steady heart. The Glimmerwood slept soundly, its memories preserved in crystalline light. Arthur Pensive, the Warden, continued his daily work—listening to the quiet symphony of his home, feeling the pulse of the earth at the cut, and offering the simple, unwavering Dot of his awareness.

But no stability is ever truly final.

Late one night, as the last of the summer warmth faded, Arthur sat at his attic window. He closed his eyes and reached out with his resonance toward the Threshold. He felt the steady hum of the Heartwood, the comforting pulse of Fig. Then, faint and distant, he felt something new in his own world—a vibration that was neither the loud chaos of the past nor the cold nothingness of the Alchemist.

It was a subtle, creeping discord.

It was a question being asked too loudly, a whisper of doubt that was beginning to echo in the hearts of the Loud Ones—a quiet, insistent pressure urging them to forget not the past, but how to dream of the future. The Great Amnesia was no longer a foe; the new struggle was a failure of the generative force of the world itself. The Dot of Belief was starting to waver.

The great work of restoration was over. The great work of inspiration was about to begin.

The Warden was needed again.

Also by Nicholas Frost

- The Boy Who Saved Christmas (Novel)

Book Two: THE GLIMMERWOOD SONG

The Balance has been restored, but a new dissonance ripples through Arthur's world. The Warden of the Balance now faces his most delicate task: saving not a forest of forgotten memories, but the source of all future dreams. When the **Dot of belief** begins to waver in the hearts of those around him, Arthur must venture beyond the Threshold again to find the lost frequency of **Inspiration**. With the help of Fig, he must learn to sing the world's quiet song, ensuring that a future worth remembering can still be created.

ACKNOWLEDGMENTS

This novel would not exist without the quiet foundations—the Dots—who helped anchor its story. My profound gratitude goes to:

- MK Storyworks, for believing in the quiet revolution of this idea and providing the structure for its reality.
- The readers and dreamers who supported my previous works, like "The Boy Who Saved Christmas."
- My family, who taught me that presence is the greatest form of kindness.
- The inspiration for Arthur, who reminded me that empathy is a resonant force, not a flaw.
- And finally, to the memory of all the forgotten moments, for proving that a simple, small stone is, in the end, the most powerful magic of all.

ABOUT THE PUBLISHER

MK Storyworks is a truly global book publisher, dedicated to the timeless mission of connecting compelling authors with enthusiastic readers across the world.

We pride ourselves on curating a diverse and dynamic list that spans the full spectrum of literary interests. Whether you are looking for an immersive escape into a bestselling fiction novel, seeking wisdom and knowledge from groundbreaking non-fiction titles, perfecting a dish with our acclaimed cookbooks, or introducing the magic of reading to the next generation with our enchanting children's books, MK Storyworks delivers stories that inform, entertain, and inspire.

Our commitment to quality, creativity, and global reach ensures that every book we publish finds its place in the hands and hearts of readers, no matter where they are.

Connect with MK Storyworks

Stay up-to-date with our latest releases, author news, and behind-the-scenes glimpses by connecting with us online:

Website: www.mkstoryworks.com

Social Media:

- YouTube: @mkstoryworks
- Instagram: @mkstoryworks
- Facebook: @mkstoryworks
- X: @mkstoryworks
- Pinterest: @mkstoryworks
- TikTok: @mkstoryworks